A LIFEGUARD'S CHOICE . . .

My head went under, and I swallowed a mouthful of water. Joy clung to me, struggling, screaming, her weight pushing me farther and farther down.

Desperate to breathe, I twisted sideways and kicked hard. My chest ached as I gasped in some air.

"Joy, listen to me!" I shouted hoarsely. "Calm down! You're okay, but Raina isn't! Raina might be dying!"

Joy clung to me, still screaming.

I glanced at Raina, floating so limply, so lifelessly in the water.

Joy's grip tightened. We started to sink again.

She'll pull us all down, I thought. All three of us will drown.

Do something!

I can't rescue them both, I realized. I have to make a choice.

Decide!

Books by R.L. Stine

Fear Street Sagas
A NEW FEAR
HOUSE OF WHISPERS
FORBIDDEN SECRETS
THE SIGN OF FEAR
THE HIDDEN EVIL
DAUGHTERS OF SILENCE
CHILDREN OF FEAR
DANCE OF DEATH
HEART OF THE HUNTER
THE AWAKENING EVIL

The Fear Street Saga
THE BETRAYAL
THE SECRET
THE BURNING
FEAR STREET SAGA
   COLLECTOR'S EDITION

The Cataluna Chronicles
THE EVIL MOON
THE DARK SECRET
THE DEADLY FIRE

Fear Park
THE FIRST SCREAM
THE LOUDEST SCREAM
THE LAST SCREAM

Fear Street Super Chillers
PARTY SUMMER
SILENT NIGHT
GOODNIGHT KISS
BROKEN HEARTS
SILENT NIGHT 2
THE DEAD LIFEGUARD
CHEERLEADERS: THE NEW EVIL
BAD MOONLIGHT
THE NEW YEAR'S PARTY
GOODNIGHT KISS 2
SILENT NIGHT 3
HIGH TIDE
SILENT NIGHT COLLECTOR'S
   EDITION
CHEERLEADERS: THE EVIL
   LIVES!

Fear Street Cheerleaders
THE FIRST EVIL
THE SECOND EVIL
THE THIRD EVIL

99 Fear Street: The House of Evil
THE FIRST HORROR
THE SECOND HORROR
THE THIRD HORROR

Available from ARCHWAY Paperbacks

FEAR STREET®
SUPER CHILLER
R·L·STINE

High Tide

A Parachute Press Book

AN ARCHWAY PAPERBACK
Published by POCKET BOOKS
New York   London   Toronto   Sydney   Tokyo   Singapore

This book is a work of fiction. Names, characters, places and incidents are products of the author's imagination or are used fictitiously. Any resemblance to actual events or locales or persons, living or dead, is entirely coincidental.

AN ARCHWAY PAPERBACK *Original*

An Archway Paperback published by
POCKET BOOKS, a division of Simon & Schuster Inc.
1230 Avenue of the Americas, New York, NY 10020

Copyright © 1997 by Parachute Press, Inc.

ISBN: 0-671-52971-4

First Archway Paperback printing June 1997

10 9 8 7 6 5 4

FEAR STREET is a registered trademark of Parachute Press, Inc.

AN ARCHWAY PAPERBACK and colophon are registered trademarks of Simon & Schuster Inc.

Cover art by Bill Schmidt

Printed in the U.S.A.

IL 7+

PART ONE

PART ONE

Chapter 1

ADAM

"Let's go, Adam!" Mitzi cried. "Let's really move this thing!"

"You want fast?" I hollered over the roar of the water scooter. "You got it!"

Laughing, I spun the scooter in a wide curve—away from the docks of Logan Beach and farther out into the ocean.

Glancing back, I saw the tall lifeguard chair looming up out of the long stretch of white sand. Twenty minutes until I have to be on duty, I thought. Plenty of time to give Mitzi the ride of her life.

"Hurry up, Adam!" Mitzi shrieked in my ear. "I want to feel this thing fly!"

I laughed again. Talk about a great summer!

Lifeguarding was hard, hot work, but totally worth it. After all, it's how I met Mitzi. The day I spotted her walking by the lifeguard station, I practically drooled.

Long blond hair, legs that went on forever, and a smile that almost knocked me out of the chair.

And now here she was, riding behind me on the water scooter, her arms wrapped around my waist.

As I said, a great summer.

I took the scooter a little father out, then revved the engine and tore across the water. We bounced and rocked, zipping back and forth under the hot sun, laughing every time a big wave tried to slap us sideways.

I could have done it all afternoon.

But I had only ten more minutes before my shift on the beach.

"One more pass!" I yelled to Mitzi. "Then we'll have to take it in so I can go to work!"

"Okay, but can we do this again tomorrow?" she yelled back.

"Sure!"

"And after you're through working, let's get a hamburger!"

"Sure!" I repeated with a grin. "Then what?"

"Then let's take a long walk on the beach, under the moonlight," she suggested with a laugh.

As Mitzi squeezed me tightly, I grinned again.

Did I say "great" summer?

Make that *excellent!*

"Hang on!" I cried. Turning again, I pointed the scooter toward the docks. Then I let it rip.

As the scooter roared across the water, Mitzi tightened her arms around me and shrieked with laughter. She leaned her head against my back, and I felt her blond hair whipping around my neck.

When we were halfway back to the docks, I spotted a huge wave rising up on our left. "Look out!" I shouted. "We're in for a soaking!"

I gunned the engine, hoping to get past the highest part of the wave before it tumbled down on us.

The wave curled higher.

Mitzi squeezed me tighter.

"Whoooooooaaa!" The wave slammed down.

We beat it by a split second!

As we slapped over the tail end of it, Mitzi's arms suddenly dropped from around my waist. Over the roar of the scooter I heard a loud splash behind me.

Girl overboard! I thought. Adam Malfitano to the rescue!

I whirled the water scooter around in a tight circle and started back to pick her up.

Through the spray of water, I saw Mitzi's blond head bob out of the frothing ocean.

Nooooo!

Too close! Too close to me!

I couldn't stop in time.

I cut back on the power and swerved to the side.

Too late!

The scooter bumped wildly as it rolled over Mitzi's thrashing body.

"Nooo!" I opened my mouth in a wail of horror.

I spun the scooter around and gaped as a dark red stain spread out over the water.

Blood.

Mitzi's blood.

Turning the foamy waves pink.

Darkening the blue-gray water. Spreading out . . . spreading . . . spreading . . .

"Nooo!" I screamed again. "Mitzi!"

I leapt off the water scooter into the cold, churning waters.

Another wave tumbled over me. It shot me away from her, toward the shore. I fought the pull of the current and struggled to plow my way toward Mitzi.

It took only a couple of strokes to reach her. She thrashed frantically, trying to keep her head above the water. I gasped.

Streams of blood criss-crossed her face. Blood gushing from a jagged wound in her forehead.

Her eyes wide with terror and pain, Mitzi opened her mouth to scream. Instead, she gulped water and began to sink again.

I reached down and grabbed her arm to haul her up. Her arm was slick with blood, but I managed to pull her head above the water.

Panicked, she threw her bloody arms around my neck—and started to drag me under.

I yanked free, grabbed her around the waist, and hauled her up again.

She kept fighting, spattering blood across my face. Her fist slammed into the side of my head.

I lost my grip on her.

I'll never be able to get her ashore! I thought.

I have to find help!

A boat, I thought. A surfer or a swimmer. Somebody has to be out here to help us!

Somebody!

Blinking the blood and salt water from my eyes, I whirled around and gazed across the tossing ocean.

And screamed in terror as a dark shape loomed up in front of me.

Chapter 2

The water scooter!

It spun around.

And now it was roaring at me!

The sound echoed like thunder as it sped through the rippling water. But there was something wrong. Horribly wrong. The protective hull of the scooter had cracked open—and the propellor was exposed.

Its deadly blades sliced the waves in half, coming at me like sharp knives.

"Nooo!" I let out a shriek—and dove aside.

Too late.

Pain shot through me as the scooter roared by.

My leg! It sliced through my leg!

I screamed in agony and swallowed a mouthful of water. Choking, I sank below the surface, then fought my way back up.

The water scooter had turned. It was coming back!

I had to get out of there before it shredded me to hamburger!

Gasping and dazed with pain, I spun around, looking for Mitzi.

I spotted her blood-streaked face bobbing out of the water. The roar of the water scooter filled my ears again. Grew louder. Louder.

The scooter was roaring back at me!

My left leg hung useless, throbbing and bleeding. I kicked with my right leg and tried to drag myself out of the path of the scooter.

But it came too fast, racing toward me like some kind of evil monster.

I thrashed my arms desperately.

Kicked with my good leg.

Tried to pull myself out of its way again.

But the scooter moved too fast. It cut into my arm. Its monstrous roar drowned out my screams.

Pain shot through my body. The scooter was on me again.

Again.

Cutting into my other arm. My back. Slicing across my shoulders.

I kept screaming as the scooter roared back and forth, cutting me every time it rolled over me.

"Adam! Help me!" Mitzi gasped and choked as she fought to keep her head above the water. "Please— help me!"

Her head went under, then bobbed up again. "Adam, help! Help me!"

The water scooter roar grew louder, drowning out Mitzi's cries.

Panicked and shivering with pain, I stretched an

arm out and dragged myself through the churning, blood-soaked waves.

As I grabbed onto her shoulder, Mitzi wrapped her arms around my neck. "Help me!" she begged. "Get me out of here, Adam! Help me before . . . before . . ."

But I couldn't help her. I could barely stay afloat.

All we could do was cling together as the roar of the water scooter grew louder and closer.

"Adam!" Mitzi cried my name once more. Then the bloody, foaming water surged into her mouth.

The water lapped at my chin, over my lips. I tilted my head back and dragged air in through my nose.

Holding tightly to each other, Mitzi and I sank beneath the surface of the ocean.

The sound of the water scooter faded.

Mitzi and I sank down. So quiet down here. So dark and quiet . . .

So this is what it feels like to drown.

Chapter 3

"We'll die!" I shouted. "We're drowning!"

"Adam!" a voice cried out.

"We're drowning. We're dying!" I yelled.

Someone grabbed my shoulder and shook it hard. "Adam!" the voice repeated. "Wake up, man! Wake up! You're having a nightmare!"

Gasping for air, I snapped my eyes open and stared up at Ian. Ian Schultz. My roommate.

Ian gazed back at me, his features twisted in worry and surprise.

"You awake now, Adam? You okay?"

I sat up and glanced around. My heart still hammered, but it slowed down when I realized exactly where I was.

In my bed. My apartment. The same apartment I'd shared with Ian last summer.

A cool ocean breeze blew in the window. The sky outside was kind of a pearly gray, the way it gets just before the sun comes up.

I could hear waves lapping against the shore, and gulls already shrieking as they started to search for food.

Normal sounds. Everything normal.

Ian ran a hand through his tangled, sandy hair and blinked at me. "It was the same nightmare, wasn't it?"

I took a shaky breath and nodded. "Yeah. Mitzi and I get ripped up by the scooter. And then we're sinking, going farther and farther under the water. Everything's black, and I can't breathe!"

I shuddered.

The nightmare had started last summer, right after Mitzi died. We'd gone out on the water scooter together, just as in the dream. She fell off. And as I spun the scooter around, it slammed into Mitzi—hard. It tore open her forehead. Fractured her skull.

Poor Mitzi.

I tried to save her, but I couldn't.

Mitzi drowned.

But in my dream I always die too. In my dream, the water scooter always goes berserk. It comes after me like some kind of monster.

"It's so real, every time I have it," I muttered, still sweating from the horrible nightmare. "It's so real. When is it going to go away? Will I have it my whole life?"

"I don't know, man." Ian rubbed his face and yawned.

He works in a boat-rental shop, but he had the day off. I knew he'd planned to sleep late. "But maybe you should think about switching psychiatrists."

"Huh? Why should I do that?" I asked. "Dr. Thall seems okay to me."

"Yeah, well, you've been seeing him for almost a year and you're still having the nightmares," Ian pointed out.

"I know, but—"

"Besides," Ian interrupted. "I've seen the guy on TV. He's on a talk show almost every other day."

"So what?" I asked. "He's got all these new ideas about treating people, and he wrote a book about it."

"I know, and he seems to have some really wacko treatments, if you ask me." Ian shrugged and yawned again. "Anyway, it's only six o'clock, and since today's my day off, I'm going back to sleep."

He narrowed his eyes at me. "What about you? You don't have to be on duty until this afternoon. You going to catch some more zzz's?"

"Maybe."

Actually, I was afraid to go back to sleep. Maybe I'd just get up and take a walk on the beach. Or ride one of the biking trails.

Anything to keep from sinking into that nightmare again.

I stretched my arms, then rubbed my eyes. I took hold of the sheet and started to throw it off.

And froze in terror.

"Nooo!" I screamed. "No! Ian, look!"

12

"What?" Ian spun around, fear in his eyes. "What is it? What's going on?"

"My legs!" I shrieked.

I pointed at the bed, where my legs should have been. "They're gone! My legs are gone! Help me! Ian—where is the rest of me?"

HIGH TIDE

Chapter 4

Staring hard at me, Dr. Thall leaned forward and put his elbows on the desk. He's a short, thin, middle-aged man with a bald head and a feeble chin.

But his blue eyes are like lasers.

"And so, Adam, you thought your legs were gone?" he asked quietly.

"Yes." I forced myself not to shudder as I remembered that moment—remembered looking down to the foot of the bed and seeing nothing but empty space where my legs should have been.

"Of course, my legs—they were under the sheet," I said. "I was perfectly okay."

"You haven't had any hallucinations in several weeks," Dr. Thall commented, shaking his head.

"I know." The last time I had one, I thought my arms were gone. And before that, my eyes.

That was the worst, thinking a fish had eaten the eyeballs out of my head.

But Dr. Thall was right—the hallucinations had stopped three weeks ago. Until this morning.

Dr. Thall rubbed his chin and frowned. "Has anything happened recently to upset you, Adam? Is anything new troubling you?"

I closed my eyes and tried to think. My first year of college had ended two weeks ago. I went home to Shadyside for a week. Nothing special happened there. After seeing all my old high school friends, I packed up and came to start work at Logan Beach.

I opened my eyes. Dr. Thall still stared hard at me, studying me.

"Maybe it's summer," I suggested. "You know. Being back on the beach again."

"If that's what is causing you to see things, maybe you should give up being a lifeguard," the doctor suggested, studying my face.

"No." I stood up and jammed my hands into the pockets of my shorts.

"Just think about it," he urged me. "It's possible that being back on the beach is too distressing for you. Perhaps you need to find a job somewhere else. In a different town. Indoors, perhaps."

"No," I repeated. I shook my head and began to pace around his office. "I have to face it. I have to conquer it. Mitzi died last summer. It was an accident. A horrible accident. I lost control of the water scooter, and she died."

"And you blamed yourself," Dr. Thall added.

"You know I did," I told him. "Anybody would. I

mean, I was driving the scooter. I felt guilty for a long time."

I stopped in front of his desk and stared at him. "But I don't blame myself anymore."

"All right, Adam. But something is still bothering you," he pointed out. "Something is still troubling your mind. Isn't that obvious to you?"

"Sure," I replied. "But what am I supposed to do—keep away from beaches for the rest of my life?" I shook my head again. "No. I have to stay here. I have no choice. I have to face my fears," I insisted.

He nodded. "Very well. I can see you're determined to stay, and I'm not going to try to stop you. I'm glad you aren't taking the blame for the accident anymore." He frowned again and leaned back in his chair. "Now. Why do you suppose you had a hallucination after so long?"

I shrugged. "All I can think of is that I'm back at the beach. The same beach where it happened. I'm even in the same apartment, with the same roommate. It makes sense, doesn't it?"

"To have nightmares—yes," he agreed. "But, frankly, the hallucination surprises me."

"You and me both," I muttered. "But maybe it was just this one time. The shock of being back, as I said. Maybe I won't see any more crazy things."

"Maybe not," he said softly. "Just be sure to stay aware, Adam."

"What do you mean?"

"You have to listen to your subconcious mind." He tapped his fingers on the desk and glanced at me sharply. "It may be trying to tell you something. I think there is something inside your brain struggling to get out."

"Like what?"

Dr. Thall smiled. "That's what we're here to find out. Now, let's get to work."

Half an hour later I stepped out of Dr. Thall's office and stopped at the receptionist's desk.

"Same time next week?" she asked cheerfully.

I nodded. And the week after, and the week after that, I thought.

Would I be seeing Thall for the rest of my life? Trying to figure out what my stupid subconscious mind was trying to tell me?

I sighed, then glanced at my watch. I had to be on beach duty soon. Dr. Thall's office was half a mile from the beach, but if I hurried, I could make it.

I'd *better* make it, I thought. I took the appointment card the receptionist handed me. If I'm late, Sean will probably get in my face.

Sean Cavanna is another lifeguard, and we're usually on duty together. He's okay, I guess. He talks a lot, and he likes to joke around.

But he also gripes a lot. And sometimes he gets in these really bad moods. His dark eyes turn as cold and mean as a shark's, and he looks ready to explode.

Being late wouldn't make him explode, but it would definitely make him gripe. And after the nightmare and the hallucination, I didn't feel like listening to him complain and carry on.

I shoved the appointment card in my pocket, picked up my duffel bag, and hurried out the door.

I walked through the streets of Logan Beach

Village, then finally reached Main Street. Across from it stood the boardwalk, then the beach.

As I started to cross the street, someone called my name.

I spun around and saw Leslie Jordan standing in front of the coffee shop where she works.

Leslie is the girl I've been going out with this summer. She's smart and good-looking, with dark brown hair and serious gray eyes.

"Hi," Leslie said, crossing the street to greet me. "I'm on a break right now. Are you on your way to work?"

I nodded, glad to see her. "Another tough day at work. Working on my tan," I joked.

"Lucky you." She took my hand and we crossed over to the boardwalk. "Want to sit down for a minute?"

I checked my watch. I still had time. "Sure." I sat down on one of the wooden benches that line the boardwalk and pulled Leslie down beside me.

"I wish we could sit here all day," she said as I slid my arm around her shoulders. "Too bad we both have to work."

"Yeah, I wouldn't mind being a beach bum," I agreed. "Swim a little. Lie in the sun. Look for seashells. Swim some more. Eat. Then go to sleep."

"Then get up and do the same thing all over again." Leslie laughed. "Sounds great."

"Come on—you'd get bored," I replied. Leslie is definitely not the lazy type.

"Maybe," she agreed. "But not for a few days, at least."

I laughed, then checked the time. "Uh-oh. I've got

18

to go. Sean is probably timing me down to the split second."

Leslie sighed and stood up. "I'll call you, okay?"

"Great." I gave her a quick kiss, then turned toward the steps that led down to the beach.

The sun bounced off the white sand, blinding me so much that I stumbled. Squinting, I fished in my pocket for my sunglasses and started to put them on.

That's when I saw her.

She stood in the sand, leaning against the step railing and gazing out toward the ocean. Her back was to me, so I couldn't see her face. But I didn't have to.

I would have known her anywhere.

That bright blond hair blowing across her back.

Those long, long legs.

The blue beaded bracelet on her left wrist. The same bracelet she wore that day last summer when we went out on the water scooter.

Mitzi.

She's not dead! I saw. The whole thing has been a nightmare—the accident, the guilt, the dreams. It's all been part of a nightmare, and I'm finally waking up. Mitzi's not dead!

"Mitzi!" I cried, running down the steps. "You're here! Mitzi!"

She pushed away from the railing and turned toward me. A gust of wind blew her hair across her face. She lifted her hand and brushed it away.

And I froze, staring in horror.

Empty eye sockets stared back at me.

Dark, empty holes in a gray-white skull.

A skull. A skeleton's head, with strips of gray flesh dangling from the gleaming bone.

Shredded, rotting flesh.

19

"Nooo!" A hoarse cry escaped my throat. "Mitzi!"

Mitzi cocked her head. Her rotting lips, black and peeling, drew back, exposing jagged, broken teeth.

"Nooooooo!" I moaned again.

The jaw of her skull creaked open, and Mitzi stared at me with empty eyes, grinning a hideous grin.

PART TWO

Chapter 5

SEAN

I glanced down from the lifeguard chair and frowned. On the sand below, Alyce Serkin stuck a tube of sunscreen into her orange beach bag. Then she stood up and began to shake the sand from her beach towel.

Alyce is a major babe. She is *hot!* To tell the truth, she's the only reason I keep this lifeguard job. So I can sit up high and stare at her all day.

She's packing up to leave, I thought. I'd better hurry.

I scanned the ocean, checking for people in trouble. Nobody needed my help. So I swung myself out of the chair and began climbing down the ladder.

Alyce didn't notice me. She stuffed the towel into her bag, then picked up a plastic bottle of water and took a drink.

I leapt off the ladder, landing quietly in the soft sand. Grinning to myself, I crept up behind Alyce and grabbed her around the waist.

She squealed—and the bottle of water went flying through the air.

I let out a laugh, squeezed her against me, and kissed the back of her neck. "Guess who?" I whispered.

"I don't have to guess!" Alyce sputtered. She tried to pull away, but I held on tight and kissed her again. "Let go of me, Sean! You really are an animal."

"You love it!" I insisted. I turned her around and kissed her on the mouth. "You know you love it."

"I do *not* love it!" she snarled. She shoved me away and scowled at me.

I reached for her, but she hopped backward. "Oh, you want me to chase you?" I asked.

"Hardly." She made a disgusted face. "Don't you get it? I don't like being grabbed like that."

"Like what?" I asked, grinning. "You want me to grab you some other way? Show me how, babe!"

"Give me a break." She rolled her eyes and picked up a floppy straw hat. "I'm leaving," she announced, pulling the hat over her curly red hair. "The sun is getting to me. And so are you."

I dropped to my knees in the sand and clasped my hands together. "Please, please, don't leave!" I begged, putting a woeful expression on my face. "I'll be good. I promise!"

Alyce rolled her eyes again. "You're hopeless."

"Exactly!" I cried. "Without you, babe, I'm totally hopeless!"

I jumped to my feet and held out my arms, but Alyce just shook her head. "I really have to go, Sean."

"Okay, okay, I give up. For now," I added. I picked up the empty water bottle and tossed it in the wire barrel next to the lifeguard station. "So," I said as Alyce zipped her beach bag. "Are we going out tonight?"

"I'm sorry. I can't." She slung the bag over her shoulder. "I've got something else I have to do."

"Yeah? What?" I asked.

Alyce's face turned pink, and it wasn't from the sun. "I'm just busy, that's all," she muttered.

Something started to sizzle inside me. I really hate being lied to. And Alyce was definitely lying. "Busy doing what?" I demanded.

"Is it any of *your* business?" she snapped.

That sizzling feeling grew stronger. As she turned and started to walk away, I grabbed her arm and spun her around so fast, her hat fell off. "I'd better not see you out with another guy," I warned.

"Hey!" Glaring, Alyce tried to yank her arm away, but I held on. "You don't own me, Sean," she declared. "Stop being such a creep."

"I'm warning you. I see you out with another guy, I'll kill him," I promised, giving her arm a shake. "I really will."

Alyce peeled my fingers off her arm. "At least you're not too possessive or anything," she said sarcastically. "If I thought you were serious . . ."

"Try me," I warned. "Just try me."

Get a grip, I told myself. I didn't want to scare Alyce. I wanted to scare away any guy who might think of going out with her.

I snatched up her hat and stuck it on my head. "How do I look?" I asked, turning sideways and striking a Mister Muscle pose.

25

"Ridiculous." She reached for the hat.

I jumped away and struck another pose. "Got a camera?" I asked. "You can get a shot for your scrapbook."

"Sure, like I'd really want one." Alyce reached for the hat again and missed. "Come on, Sean. Give it to me."

"Say please!" Laughing, I ducked away. Then I took the hat off and sailed it to her like a Frisbee. As I did, I caught a glimpse of my watch. Five minutes after one. "Hey, where's Adam?" I asked, glancing around.

Alyce shrugged. "How should I know?"

"I'm supposed to be on a break," I told her. "That guy is always late."

"You mean you're *not* on your break?" she asked, jamming the hat back on her head. "I don't believe it! Some lifeguard you are—you're not even watching the swimmers!"

I grinned. "That's because I can't take my eyes off you, Alyce!"

"Honestly, Sean! You really are a pig!" She hitched her duffel bag onto her shoulder and started to march away.

I watched her for a moment. What a great walk!

Then I ran up behind her and grabbed her around the waist. "Gotcha again!" I cackled.

Alyce yelped in surprise. Then she began to struggle. "Let go of me!" she cried. "Sean, this isn't funny!"

She's not really angry, I told myself. She's crazy about me, right? Right.

As I bent to kiss her, a piece of straw from her hat stabbed me in the eye. I hollered, stumbled backward, and bumped into somebody.

"Hey, why don't you watch where you're going?" I snapped. Rubbing my eye, I whirled around and found myself staring at Adam Malfitano.

"What's going on?" Adam asked, gazing at my watery eye.

"Sean was being his usual gross self, and he got attacked by my hat," Alyce declared angrily. "Serves him right."

Adam ran a hand through his brown hair and flashed Alyce a big, goofy smile. I didn't like the look on his face.

The *admiring* look.

"You're late," I told him. "Where have you been?"

He dragged his eyes away from Alyce. "Sorry," he told me. "I had to see my doctor."

"What's wrong?" Alyce asked, sounding concerned.

Now he's trying for her sympathy, I thought in disgust. Still rubbing my eye, I turned away.

As I stared out across the breaking waves, my heart suddenly began to pound. I sucked in my breath and grabbed Adam's arm.

"Nooo!" I moaned. I pointed to the water. "Shark! Shark got that girl!"

Chapter 6

"Where?" Adam cried in a frantic voice, his head swiveling back and forth. "Sean—where?"

"Out there!" I shouted. "Can't you see all the blood in the water?"

Adam froze. He didn't even bother to look where I was pointing. Instead, he stared at me, and his brown eyes got real wide.

"I'll get . . . I'll get the . . ." Adam's voice shook. "I'll get the . . . life preserver."

But he didn't move. His lips were almost as white as his face.

Talk about freaked! I thought. The guy's about to pass out!

Actually, it would have been fun to see if he'd really keel over in a dead faint. But then I'd be stuck taking care of the poor guy.

28

"Hey, man, get a grip!" I told him. "I was just goofing!"

He blinked and licked his lips again. "You were what?"

"Goofing," I repeated. Laughing, I dragged him around so he faced the ocean. "See? No sharks out there. Nobody getting chomped to pieces. It was a joke, get it? A dumb joke."

"Dumb is right!" Alyce declared. "Honestly, Sean! What did you do, leave your brain at home today?"

I shrugged. "Hey, I can't help it. I've got a crazy sense of humor."

Alyce rolled her eyes, then turned sympathetically to Adam. "Are you okay? You look a little pale."

"I'm fine." Adam smiled at her. "Embarrassed though. I guess I kind of overreacted."

"Well, no wonder! I mean, after what happened last summer!" she exclaimed.

"Oh, good, Alyce," I told her. "Remind him of it all over again."

"You're the one who reminded him," she shot back. "Talking about blood in the water."

"Hey, it's okay," Adam insisted. "Really."

"Well, anyway, don't pay any attention to Sean," Alyce told him, smiling again. "He's the only one here who thinks he's funny."

"It's true," I agreed sadly. "My comic genius is totally misunderstood."

Alyce groaned. "Like I said, Adam, don't pay any attention to him." With another scowl at me, she began to stride away.

"Don't forget!" I called after her. "Eight tonight!"

Alyce whirled around. "What about it?"

"You and me, babe," I reminded her. "I'll be coming by your cottage, so leave the porch light on."

"Okay," she agreed. "But I won't be there. I can't see you tonight, remember?"

Before I could answer, Alyce gave Adam a wink and a little wave. Then she turned and walked across the sand toward the boardwalk.

I faked a laugh. "She doesn't mean it, you know," I told Adam. "She'll be home waiting for me tonight. You can count on it."

"Sure." Adam didn't look at me. He kept his eyes on Alyce as she picked her way through all the sunbathers and sand buckets.

And he was smiling.

"What's so funny?" I demanded.

"Huh? Nothing." He glanced up at the lifeguard station. It's a tall wooden platform with a railing around it and two lifeguard chairs on top. "Whoa!" he said. "We'd better get up there fast. We're on duty."

Slinging his beach bag over his shoulder, Adam sprinted up the steps to the wooden platform. As I followed, that sizzling feeling started up again in the pit of my stomach.

Ignore it, I told myself. Don't let it get to you. Alyce will be there tonight.

Won't she?

Before I sat down in the lifeguard chair, I glanced toward the boardwalk. In the distance, I spotted Alyce's floppy straw hat growing smaller and smaller as she walked away.

"I know she's awesome-looking, but you'd better take your eyes off her—for a while anyway," Adam scolded, following my gaze. "We've got swimmers to watch."

"Yeah." I put on a T-shirt and my sunglasses, then sat down. "I just wish I could keep an eye on her all the time," I admitted.

He chuckled. "I don't think Alyce would like that too much."

"I guess not." I gazed out at the ocean and sighed. "I can't help it though. I get jealous sometimes."

"So? Everybody gets a little jealous once in a while," Adam said, smearing sunscreen on his nose. "It's normal, right?"

"I'm not talking about a 'little,' " I declared. "I'm talking big-time jealous. You want an example?"

He shrugged. "Sure."

"There was this girl I went with back in high school," I told him. "Cindy. Funny, sexy, a great dancer. Crazy about me," I added. "At least I thought she was. I actually thought we'd be together forever."

My heart started pounding, and I realized my hands were clenched into fists. I guess it doesn't matter how much time goes by. Whenever I think about her, I start to burn.

"So what happened?" Adam asked.

I took a deep breath. "She sneaked out on me with another guy," I replied. "We were supposed to go to the movies, but at the last minute she said she had something else to do."

Just like Alyce, I thought.

"I knew she was lying," I went on. "You can always tell, right?"

Adam shook his head.

"Well, *I* can," I told him. "Anyway, I followed her, just to make sure."

"You're kidding. You really followed her?"

"Sure I did," I declared. "I had to find out what was going on, didn't I?"

"I guess," Adam said doubtfully.

"Anyway, I saw her meet up with this guy from school," I went on. "She gave him a big kiss, then hopped into his car. They spent three hours at the amusement park, going on rides, holding hands. Kissing."

"Wait a sec." Adam stared at me, his eyes questioning me. "You mean you followed them there? You stayed there the whole time?"

"Yeah. I was burning up," I told him. "Ready to explode. You know what I mean?"

"Maybe. I mean, I get angry sometimes," he said.

"Not angry, Adam." I clenched my fists even tighter. "Furious, wild—"

"Okay, I get the picture," he interrupted.

"Yeah? Well, let me finish," I insisted. "See, you probably think I was angry at Cindy. And I was. But the one I wanted to get was the guy. Jay. So I did. I started out slow at first."

Adam stood up and leaned against the platform railing. "Look, I don't think I want to hear this."

"But I want to tell you." I climbed up too, and stood next to him. "Hey, we're stuck on this platform together for three more hours. As long as nobody starts to drown or something, you might as well listen."

I nudged him in the arm. "Who knows? You might learn something."

Adam stayed quiet, staring out at the swimmers.

"Like I said, I started out slow," I continued. "I put

a note in Jay's locker, letting him know I'd seen him with Cindy. Then I cornered him in the locker room and told him he'd be sorry.

"Later I bumped into him in the hall. Said I was after him. Warned him to be ready."

"That's starting out slow?" Adam asked sarcastically.

I shrugged. "For me it was. Remember, I felt like I had a time bomb inside me. Tick, tick, tick."

I gripped the railing hard, and my knuckles turned white. "Okay. Ready for the end of the story?"

Adam kept staring out at the water. He's probably wishing something would happen out there, I thought. Something to stop me from talking.

I didn't blame him. I wasn't exactly crazy about the story myself. But I had to tell it to him.

I had to!

"Well, Jay didn't believe I was out to get him," I went on. "I mean, all I did was shoot my mouth off. And after a while he figured I wasn't serious. Naturally, he figured wrong."

"Get to the point." Adam sighed impatiently. "What happened?"

"One day I took him out to the woods. And I beat him up. He wasn't ready, see? He didn't think I was serious. But I was!" I declared loudly. "And the more he screamed, the harder I beat him! I beat him so bad, he almost died!"

The blood pounded in my head, and my breath came faster and faster.

"Hey, Sean, take it easy," Adam murmured nervously.

"I can't," I told him. "It happened two years ago,

33

but I can see it like it was yesterday. Jay's bloody face. My fists pounding on him until they were raw and bloody too. I scared myself, I was so out of control!"

I took a deep breath. Then another. My breathing finally slowed, and my heart stopped thundering.

"I think that's why I'm a lifeguard," I said. "Because if I wasn't saving lives, I'd be *taking* lives. Sometimes I just can't control how angry I get."

Adam didn't say anything at first. He blew his whistle at some kids kicking sand at each other. Then he pushed away from the railing.

I heard him flop down in his chair and let out a big breath. "Hey, Sean," he finally said. "Why did you tell me that story?"

"Simple," I replied. I turned around and peered at him over the top of my shades. "Because I saw the way you were looking at Alyce."

Chapter 7

ADAM

*L*ater, as I trotted up the stairs to my apartment, I kept hearing Sean's voice in my head. *I saw the way you were looking at Alyce.*

And I kept picturing that other guy—Jay—the one Sean beat to a pulp. Or so he said.

Did he really do it? I wondered.

Sean liked to play jokes. Maybe this was just a joke. Tell Adam a gory whopper and watch the sucker fall for it.

But somehow I didn't think he was kidding around. Not this time.

I watched his face when he was telling me. Nobody could fake that look. Dark eyes shooting sparks. Lips twisted in anger. Furious, as he said. Wild.

And his hands. Bunched into fists. Gripping the wooden rail as if he wanted to rip it off. He could do it too. He's definitely got the muscles to rip that railing off and bash somebody with it.

No, not just somebody, I reminded myself. I'm the one he wanted to bash. I'm the one he was warning.

Because he didn't like the way I looked at Alyce.

As I reached the apartment door, I tried to shake the images away. Forget about Sean, I thought. I can't let him get to me. I have better things to think about. Better things to do.

Especially tonight.

Smiling at the thought of tonight's plans, I opened the door and stepped inside the apartment. It's on the second floor of a two-story bungalow, and it's kind of small—one bedroom, a bathroom, and a long living room with a kitchen at one end. But it's close to the beach, and it has a balcony with a great view of the dunes.

Ian sat on the couch, flipping through a sports magazine. "Perfect timing," he said as I came in. "I ordered a pizza. It should be here any second."

"Great. I'm starving." Dropping my beach bag, I kicked off my flip-flops and padded over to the couch. "So what did you do on your day off?"

"What do you think?" Ian grinned. "I checked out the beach."

I grinned back. "You checked out all the *females* at the beach, you mean."

"Not all. Just the young, good-looking ones."

I laughed. "Find any?"

"Dozens. Hundreds!"

I laughed again. Ian is definitely girl crazy. "And did you manage to find someone to go out with?" I asked. "Or did they all turn you down?"

Before Ian could answer, someone knocked at the door. "Food!" Ian cried, leaping up to answer it. He paid the delivery boy, then brought the extra-large pizza box over to the coffee table.

My stomach rumbled at the smell of cheese and pepperoni. I ate two slices fast, then went to the kitchen for something to drink.

"This thing is practically empty," I complained as I stared into the refrigerator. "Whose turn is it to buy food anyway?"

"Okay, okay, it's mine," Ian admitted. "But I sprang for dinner, didn't I?" He waved a piece of pizza crust in the air. "I get paid in a couple of days. I'll buy stuff then."

I laughed. "I'll starve to death first. Don't tell me you spent your last dime on the pizza."

Ian shook his head. "No. But I need the rest of my money for tonight."

"Ah-ha!" I cried. "Does that mean you *did* manage to get a date?"

"What do you think?" Grinning again, Ian glanced at his watch. "Whoa! I'd better get moving." He tossed the crust into the pizza box and hurried out of the living room.

As I pulled out a carton of orange juice, I heard the shower running. "Hey, don't take too long, man!" I hollered. "I want to get in there too. And don't use up all the hot water!"

"What's the rush?" Ian shouted back.

"I'm going out tonight!" I chugged the last of the juice and walked back to the couch.

"So am I, remember?" he called out.

The shower continued for a few more minutes. As I

ate a third slice of pizza, I heard the bathroom door open. "You don't need your car, do you?" Ian called from the bedroom.

"I don't think so. Why?" I asked.

"Because I need wheels. Okay to borrow yours?"

"Again?" I asked. "Ian, you borrow my car every night. I haven't seen it in weeks."

"Aww—it misses you too," Ian joked.

I shook my head and kept eating the pizza. Ian has a habit of borrowing my stuff. Car, towels, money, CDs—you name it, he borrows it.

"So, can I use it tonight?" Ian asked. "It's really important."

"Okay, okay," I grumbled. After all, I really didn't need it.

"Thanks. You won't regret it," he told me. "I'll even fill it up."

"You'd better," I warned as he walked into the living room. "The last time you—" I broke off, staring at him.

Ian stood in front of the couch, pulling on a T-shirt that matched his light blue eyes. As I watched, he started tucking the shirt into a pair of black jeans.

"What's wrong?" he asked, noticing my stare.

I scowled at him. "Aren't those my jeans?"

He grinned and finger-combed his sandy blond hair. "Yeah. A perfect fit. Nice and soft too."

"Thanks," I said sarcastically. "I'm really glad you approve."

He laughed. "Admit it, Adam, these jeans look better on me. Besides, I've got a date with a really hot girl I met on the beach."

"Guess what? So do I," I told him.

"Yeah, but . . . huh?" Ian gaped at me, totally

shocked. "You mean you're not going out with Leslie?"

I shook my head. "Hey, it's not like Leslie and I are engaged or anything," I declared.

"Sure, but you know how jealous she gets," Ian reminded me. "Remember that time she called and *my* date answered? Leslie was positive you had a girl over here and she went ballistic."

I nodded. Leslie definitely had a temper. "I'm still going tonight," I told him. "It's just one date."

"Okay, but you'd better hope Leslie doesn't find out about it," he warned me.

I rolled my eyes. "Thanks for the advice, *Mom.*" Tossing the pizza crust into the box, I went into the bedroom and got ready to take a shower.

As I stood under the water, washing off the sand and sunscreen, Sean's words flashed into my mind again.

I saw the way you were looking at Alyce.

I turned my face up to the hot spray, picturing the angry sparks in Sean's eyes and the way his muscles bulged as he clenched his fists.

Shaking my head, I tried to shove the warning from my mind. I'm being a wimp, I thought. Was I going to let Sean scare me? Let his crazy jealousy ruin my plans for tonight?

No way.

I've been through enough, I thought. So forget about Sean. Forget about Leslie.

It's time to have some fun.

I washed my hair, then stepped out of the shower. As I wiped the steam from the mirror, the bedroom phone rang.

"Hey . . . can you get that, Ian?" I shouted.

The phone rang again.

"Ian?"

No response.

"Ian, get the phone!" I shouted.

No reply. No footsteps.

The phone rang a fourth time.

I quickly fumbled for a towel, wrapped it around my waist, and pulled open the bathroom door.

The phone sat on a table between the two beds, ringing for the fifth time.

But I didn't pick it up.

I didn't move. I *couldn't* move.

All I could do was stare at Ian's bed.

He lay sprawled on his stomach on top of the covers, his head hanging over the edge of the mattress.

His arms were flung out from his sides.

His legs were twisted and bent at weird angles, as if someone had snapped them backward at the knee-caps.

I couldn't see his face. But I didn't need to.

Ian didn't move. He didn't twitch. His back didn't rise and fall as he breathed.

Because he wasn't breathing.

Ian was dead!

Chapter 8

*T*he room spun wildly. My stomach churned.

I swallowed hard and closed my eyes, bracing myself against the doorjamb to keep from falling.

Ian?

Ian? Dead?

Do something! I urged myself.

But what?

The phone rang again. That's it, I thought, call the cops. Call 911.

I opened my eyes.

And gasped.

Ian's body was gone.

Blinking, I stared at his bed. At his rumpled clothes, strewn across the mattress.

I shook my head and blinked again. "Ian?" All I saw were Ian's old jeans and shirt.

41

He was never there, I realized. I was staring at his clothes the whole time. Ian had hurried out to meet his date.

I was seeing things, I realized with a groan. Again. Why? Why was I suddenly doing this?

The phone rang, and I bounded across the room and snatched it up. "Hello?" I gasped.

"Adam?" Leslie asked, sounding uncertain. "Is that you?"

"Yeah." I took a shaky breath and sank down on my bed. "It's me."

"Did you just get in, or something? You sound like you've been running."

"I, uh . . . no, I was in the shower," I told her. "I heard the phone and when I came out, I . . . I thought—"

"Adam, you sound really strange," she declared. "What's wrong?"

"Uh . . ." I glanced at Ian's bed again. "Ian's clothes."

"Huh? His clothes?" Leslie's voice rose. "What are you talking about? What's going on?"

"I don't know!" I cried. I took some more deep breaths. "Sorry, but when I came out of the shower to get the phone, I saw Ian's clothes," I explained. "He tossed them on his bed when he changed . . . and I thought . . ."

"You thought what?" she asked.

"That *he* was lying there," I told her.

"So? It's evening. The room is probably all shadowy," she declared. "Your eyes played a trick on you."

"No, you don't get it, Leslie," I argued. "I really saw Ian's body. His dead body. It wasn't any optical illusion. Besides, it happened this morning too. I thought my legs were missing. I was so sure of it, I freaked out."

"Oh, Adam." Leslie sighed sympathetically. "I can't believe you're starting to see things again."

"Yeah, me either," I agreed. "Dr. Thall was surprised too."

"He should be," she muttered. "What did he have to say about it?"

"Not much," I admitted. "He thinks my subconscious mind is trying to tell me something."

She sighed again. "I'm really worried about you, Adam. And I don't think the great Dr. Thall is helping you at all. You sound really stressed."

"I am, but—"

"Want me to come over?" she asked. "I could rent a movie and bring some microwave popcorn. I can be there in twenty minutes."

"Thanks, but I'm not doing too well," I told her quickly, suddenly remembering my date later tonight. "I'd be lousy company."

"I don't mind. Really."

"I know, but I'm still feeling kind of shaky." That's definitely true, I thought. "I'm just going to lie down, okay?"

"Oh. Okay." Leslie sounded really disappointed.

"I'll call you tomorrow," I told her.

"Sure, Adam," she agreed softly. "Tomorrow."

I said good-bye and hung up.

Jerk, I told myself. You hurt her feelings.

But at least I didn't lie to her, I thought. I'm *not* doing too well. I'm seeing things that aren't really there. And I don't know why.

I really did feel shaky too, so I stretched out on my bed. But after a few minutes I sat up. Just lying there made me feel jittery. Better to keep moving, I thought.

I put on some clothes, then went back into the bathroom to brush my hair. I stared at myself in the mirror. I looked really shaken. Pale.

Get a grip, I told myself. You can't show up for your date looking as if you were being chased by aliens or something.

I went into the living room and put on a CD. The blast of music made me even more jittery. I shut it off and checked my watch.

Not quite time to go, but I decided to leave anyway. I'd walk along the boardwalk, then head into town. Maybe that would calm me down.

I hauled my duffel bag onto the couch and took out my wallet. As I checked to make sure I had enough money, my stomach growled softly. Three slices of pizza obviously wasn't enough.

The pizza was cold by now though. I stuffed the box into the trash can, then grabbed a green apple from the bowl on the kitchen counter and hurried toward the door.

As I reached for the doorknob, I raised the shiny apple to my mouth.

The apple's green skin seemed to melt.

My hand froze on the doorknob.

My heart stuttered to a stop, then began to race.

The apple's skin kept changing. Wrinkling, sagging. Melting away, until I saw what was underneath it.

A skull.

I was holding a green, rotting skull. I could smell

it. Moldy and putrid, with vacant eye sockets and shreds of skin dangling from stumps of black, twisted teeth.

As I stared in horror, the wet apple jaws began to move. "Help me, Adam!" a hoarse voice inside the apple croaked. "Help me. Don't let me drown!"

Chapter 9

SEAN

*E*asy, Sean, I told myself as I walked along the path toward Alyce's beach cottage. She'll be there. She was only kidding around this afternoon when she said she had other plans.

Wasn't she?

Sure she was. She's crazy about me! She wouldn't sneak around on me the way Cindy did.

The path curved, and I caught sight of the cottage, small and white, with blue shutters and a yellow bug light over the front door.

The light was on.

Yes! I thought with a grin. She's definitely there, waiting for me!

Some kind of red wildflower grew along the path, so I picked a fistful. Then I trotted up the wooden steps onto the front porch.

I thumped on the door and waited, still grinning.

No sound from inside. "Hey, Alyce!" I called. "It's me! Sean!"

Still no sound.

I thumped again, harder. "You asleep or something?" I shouted. "Wake up, babe! Time to party!"

Finally, I heard footsteps. I swiped my hair off my forehead and tried to arrange the flowers into a bouquet. A couple of stems broke, but they still looked pretty good.

The door opened.

Kathy, Alyce's roommate, stared out at me. She wore a bathrobe and had a towel wrapped around her head. "Oh. Sean, hi," she said. "You scared me, yelling and beating on the door like that."

"Sorry," I told her. I pulled a flower loose and held it out to her. "Here. Stick this in a vase. Every time you look at it, you'll think of me."

Kathy giggled and took the flower. "Wow. You shouldn't have." She patted the damp towel. "I better go dry my hair now."

"No problem. You want to tell Alyce I'm here?"

"Um . . ." She bit her lip. "I would, but . . . I can't."

"Excuse me?"

"I can't tell her," she repeated softly. "Alyce isn't here."

I stared at her.

"Well . . . see you, Sean." She started to shut the door.

"Wait a sec." I put my hand flat against the door to keep it open. "You mean she's not here *yet,* don't you? She ran out to do a couple of errands, right?"

"Not exactly."

"What's that supposed to mean?" I asked. "Where *exactly* is she?"

"I don't know." Kathy bit her lip and patted the towel again. "Sean, my hair is—"

"Forget about your hair!" I snapped. "I asked you where Alyce is. Now tell me!"

"I don't know!" she insisted. "She didn't tell me. She said she was going out. I think she went to the movies or something, but I'm not sure."

The sizzling feeling didn't start small this time. It was already a full-blown fire, burning inside me. Burning so fast and furiously, I couldn't speak.

Kathy stared at me for a second, then quickly shut the door.

I slapped it angrily, then spun around and leapt off the wooden porch. As I strode down the path, I realized I still held the bunch of wildflowers in my hand.

Slowly, I crushed the red blossoms between my fingers.

This is what I want to do to him, I thought. Whoever Alyce is with, I want to crush him!

With a cry of rage I tossed the red pulp against the blue door of Alyce's cottage and hurried to my car.

I'll wait outside the village movie theater, I decided as I gunned the motor and tore along the bumpy road. Wait for Alyce and her date to come out. See who the guy is.

And then I'll get him.

But it won't be like the last time, I decided. Last time I made Cindy's guy wait. Fooled him into thinking I wasn't serious. Then I pounced.

I won't play that game this time. I can't.

I was boiling inside, ready to erupt. I couldn't wait

48

days to take care of the guy. I had to do it fast or I'd explode!

Gripping the steering wheel, I swerved around a bend and aimed the car down the main street of Logan Beach. The town fills up in the summer, so the place was crowded with tourists, groups of kids, and lots of traffic.

Ahead of me, a van braked and got ready to back into a parking space. Leaning on the horn, I stepped on the gas and zipped into the space head-on.

"Hey!" The van driver, a short guy with a fat stomach, came huffing and puffing up to my window. "Didn't you see me signaling? You stole my space!"

"Yeah?" I shoved the door open and got out. "I didn't see your name on it."

"But . . . but . . ." he stammered.

"But what?" I shouted into his face. "You don't want to fight about a parking space—do you?"

"Whoa! Who said anything about fighting?" The man held up his hands and began to back away.

As I took a step toward him, he turned and scrambled back into his van.

I started after him, then stopped.

Calm down, I told myself. Don't get into it with that jerk. Save it for the other guy.

Alyce's guy.

I took a deep breath, then strode down to the drugstore that stood across from the town's only movie theater.

The lobby was empty. Good. The show wasn't over yet.

It hasn't even started, I thought with a grim smile. When the guy comes out—that's when the real show starts!

I leaned against the front of the drugstore and waited, thinking about Alyce. How could she pull something like this after I warned her about what would happen? Did she think I was kidding?

She'll see, I thought, checking my watch. Shouldn't be long now. Then she'll see that I was serious.

Dead serious.

As I glanced across at the lobby again, I suddenly tensed. People were milling around inside, heading for the doors. The movie had let out.

Come on, Alyce, I silently urged her. Come on out. Let me see the guy you're with.

The theater doors swung open, and I caught a glimpse of bright red hair shining in the lights.

Alyce.

As she stepped outside, she reached out and took the hand of the guy next to her.

I stared at his face and felt the rage inside me begin to boil faster and faster. "I don't believe it!" I muttered to myself.

"She's with *him?*"

Chapter 10

I squeezed my eyes shut. It couldn't be him! He wouldn't do this to me.

It had to be somebody else!

I snapped my eyes open and stared across the street again, hoping to see that I was wrong.

But the same guy stood next to Alyce, squeezing her hand and smiling at her.

I don't believe it, I thought again. A guy I see all the time. A friend!

No—not a friend. Somebody who only *pretended* to be my friend.

And now he's sneaking out with my girl.

"Whoa!"

My breath came hard and fast. I dug my fingernails into the palms of my hands and felt the blood pound painfully against my skull.

Get him! I thought, staring across the street. I've waited too long already.

Get him now!

As the rage inside me boiled over, I shoved away from the drugstore and charged into the street.

Get him! my mind chanted. Pound him! Pound that smile off his face!

A horn blared suddenly, close enough to make me jump. A huge truck bore down on me.

"Hey!" I let out a startled scream.

And skidded to a stop inches from its front bumper.

"Jerk!" the guy in the passenger seat called out as the truck lumbered along. "You want to get killed? Watch where you're going!"

I raced to the end of the truck, thinking to cross behind it. But a beat-up blue van rode on the truck's tail, blocking my way.

"Hey!" I shouted, kicking out at the van. "Move this thing! Step on it!"

The van crawled by. Music blared from its speakers, and the kids inside laughed as I kicked out again in frustration.

"Kick it a little harder, man!" one of the kids sneered. "Maybe you'll break your toe!"

Their laughter drifted back as the van slowly rolled by. I bunched my fists and gritted my teeth. I felt like pulling those kids out, one by one, and showing them that life isn't so funny. That life can be painful.

Save it, I reminded myself. Save it for the guy holding Alyce's hand.

Save it for the creep who pretended to be my friend.

At last the van pulled past me. I glanced over to the movie theater.

Alyce and her date were gone.

More horns blared. Headlights bore down from opposite directions. I stopped, trying to decide which way to go.

Someone shouted at me to move it.

Darting between the oncoming cars, I charged across the street and onto the sidewalk.

They couldn't have disappeared so fast, I thought. They're lost in the crowd, that's all.

I had to find them. I had to pound the guy. Teach him a lesson.

I had to get rid of the rage burning me up inside.

Frantic to find them, I craned my neck, searching for Alyce's red hair again.

I couldn't find her.

Furious, I plunged into the crowd and began to shoulder my way through. I'll get them, I told myself. I'll pay her back for this. I have to!

Still craning my neck, I collided roughly with a girl rounding the corner.

"Leslie!"

Leslie Jordan stumbled back. She had to hang on to me to keep from falling.

"What's your problem, Sean?" Leslie cried, steadying herself and rubbing her arm. "Why don't you watch where you're going? You almost knocked me down!"

"Did you see Alyce?" I demanded breathlessly. "Did you see who she's with?"

Leslie tucked her dark hair behind her ears and sighed. The light faded in her eyes. "Yes." She sighed. "I saw."

I ground my teeth together as my blood pounded harder than ever.

Leslie sighed again. "Listen, I know exactly how you feel—"

I didn't wait for her to finish. "Got to go," I muttered, charging past her down the sidewalk.

"Sean, wait!" Leslie called.

I ignored her and kept going. I had only one thing on my mind.

Find the guy.

Punch his lights out.

Teach him a lesson he'll never forget.

The crowd had thinned out and I could see better now.

But Alyce was still nowhere in sight.

I kept trotting along the sidewalk, watching both sides of the street.

Find him! I thought. Get him! Pound him!

"Whoa! Careful, man!" a boy cried out as I crashed into him. He looked to be about fifteen or sixteen.

I grabbed the front of the guy's shirt and stuck my face into his. "Why don't *you* be careful, jerk?"

The boy's eyes widened. "Sure," he agreed in a voice that cracked. "Hey, whatever you say. Sorry."

"No, you're not," I growled. "You don't know what sorry is, so I'm going to teach you!"

Clamping my hand on the back of his neck, I shoved him into a shadowy alley lined with metal trash cans. He landed on his knees with a gasp.

I yanked him to his feet, spun him around, and punched him in the face.

Blood spurted from his nose. He rocked back on his feet, then staggered into one of the trash cans. Before he hit the ground, I dragged him up again.

"Are you sorry yet?" I hissed through my teeth. "Huh?"

The blood poured over his lips and dripped from his chin. He tried to speak, but I didn't give him the chance.

I punched him in the stomach, and as he bent double, I leapt on him, rolling him to the ground.

And then I was all over him. Pounding his ribs and back. Sinking my fist into his stomach again.

"Are you sorry yet?" I kept asking. "Are you sorry?"

"Sean!"

A girl's voice behind me.

"Sean!" Leslie. "Sean, stop!"

She yanked at the back of my shirt. I shook her off, but she grabbed hold again.

"Stop! Stop!"

Leslie threw her arm around my neck and yanked my head back. "Stop it! *Stop!*" she shrieked in my ear. "You're going to *kill* him!"

Chapter 11

Crazy.

I went totally crazy last night.

Sitting in the lifeguard chair the next morning, I kept trying to concentrate on my job. Checking the beach. Watching the swimmers and the water-skiers.

But I kept flashing on the poor kid from last night. The blood gushing from his nose. The way he curled his arms around his head to protect himself. The look of pure terror in his eyes.

I was out of control. Totally nuts! That kid must have known what I was going to do. He saw it in my face. I was going to kill him.

Admit it, Sean, I thought. If Leslie hadn't been there, that kid would be lying in the alley this morning. Beaten to a pulp.

Shifting restlessly in the chair, I remembered

Leslie's arm locked around my neck. And her frantic voice shrieking in my ear.

At first I didn't even hear her words. And I tried to throw her off.

But she held on. Held on and screamed until finally I realized what I was doing. And I stopped.

Leslie finally let go of my neck and stared at me, a stunned expression on her face.

"Don't look so scared," I told her. "It's over. Really. I'm through."

"What happened?" she asked in a shaky voice. "Why were you hitting him? What did he do?"

I shook my head. I couldn't explain it. "Let's just get out of here."

Together we helped the kid to his feet. As we walked out of the alley, I slipped him fifty bucks so he'd keep his mouth shut.

I'm lucky he took it, I thought. He could have made major trouble if he wanted to.

Sighing, I shifted in the chair again. I might not be so lucky next time, I told myself. I have to control these rages! I don't want to ruin my life because of Alyce.

But the second I thought of Alyce—and her date— I felt that spark of anger inside me again.

That guy—my so-called friend—had to be taught a lesson! I couldn't let him off the hook.

He was trying to steal my girl. And he had to pay!

The spark of anger flared. Pounding my fist on the chair arm, I leapt to my feet. I couldn't sit still, not with the image of Alyce and the guy stuck in my mind. Laughing together. Holding hands!

I had to do something—anything—or I'd go nuts again.

57

With a groan I gripped the platform railing and stared out at the ocean.

The water looked like iron. Gray and hard. Rough, choppy waves crested and broke, tossing swimmers onto the shore like rag dolls.

High tide, I realized suddenly. Get the red flags posted before somebody gets killed.

Grabbing three red warning flags from the barrel on top of the lifeguard stand, I clambered down the ladder and ran to the edge of the water. I jabbed one flag into the sand, then walked several yards along the shore.

As I stuck a second flag into the sand, a girl glanced up from her beach towel. "What's that for?" she asked, squinting against the sun.

"It's a warning flag," I explained. "The tide's high right now, see?" I pointed at the waterline. "And the ocean's really rough."

She nodded. "Is everybody supposed to get out?"

"Nope. But you go in at your own risk," I told her. "When the tide's this high, the current can get very dangerous. It's incredibly strong. It'll pull you under so fast, you won't even know what hit you."

The girl gave a little shudder. "I think I'll just stay here, where it's safe, and work on my tan."

"Smart move." I worked the flag deeper into the sand so it wouldn't blow over, then started down the beach to post the third one.

About fifty yards up ahead, two girls stood at the shoreline, talking to a guy with brown hair and a Logan Beach duffel bag slung over his shoulder.

Adam Malfitano.

I stopped suddenly, watching him. He looks so

58

relaxed, I thought. Like he has nothing on his mind. Nothing to worry about.

How can he act like that?

The spark of anger flared again.

One of the girls leaned close to Adam. She must have said something funny, because he threw back his head and laughed.

As he did, he spotted me.

He didn't wave. He didn't even nod.

Instead, he quickly glanced down at the sand. Then he shuffled around a couple of steps so his back was to me, and went on chatting with the girls.

He's avoiding my stare, I thought.

He can't look me in the eye.

Is he really as cool and relaxed as he seems?

Or is it an act?

The anger burned, and I stabbed the flag into the sand so hard, I almost broke the pole.

Does Adam know how angry I am? I wondered.

Does he know how dangerous I can be when I'm feeling like this?

Chapter 12

ADAM

"This is so incredible, Adam!" Joy Bailey exclaimed. "I mean, Raina and I were actually talking about you just the other day!"

"We really were," Raina Foster agreed. "And then we run into you our very first morning here. It's totally weird, isn't it?"

"Yeah, definitely." I grinned, then glanced over my shoulder.

I watched Sean stab the warning flag into the sand. Then he straightened up and stared at me.

The scowl on Sean's face made me shudder.

He looks really wired, I thought. As if he wants to pick a fight.

As I turned back to Joy and Raina, I spotted Ian jogging toward us. Trust Ian to show up when there are pretty girls around, I thought with a smile.

"Hey, Ian," I said as he joined us. "What are you doing here?"

"It's my lunch break," he explained. "I decided to grab a hot dog and then hang out at the beach until it's time to go back to work."

He smiled at Joy and Raina, then turned back to me. "Aren't you going to introduce me?"

"Sure." I clapped him on the shoulder. "Ian Schultz, meet Joy Bailey and Raina Foster. The three of us went to Shadyside High together. We haven't seen one another since we graduated though."

"Can you believe it?" Joy asked. She has short, curly brown hair and a bouncy personality. "Our first day at Logan Beach, and it's like a reunion!"

Ian laughed and nudged me in the side. "Lucky you," he murmured.

I gave him a little shove. "Ian's my roommate," I explained to Joy and Raina.

Raina smiled at him. She's tall, with blond hair and a great figure. "Are you a lifeguard too?" she asked.

Ian shook his head. "I work at a boat-rental place down the beach."

"Ooh, I love boats!" Joy exclaimed. "Maybe we'll rent one while we're here."

Ian immediately began talking about the different kinds of boats they could rent and what it cost. While they chatted, I glanced around again.

Sean was halfway back to the lifeguard station. But as I watched, he stopped and turned around.

And stared at me again. Even from this distance, I could see that his hands were clenched into fists. And I could practically see the glare in his eyes.

I swallowed hard, remembering the story he told me about the kid he beat up in high school. Beat him almost to death because he'd sneaked out with Sean's girlfriend.

I still couldn't believe it. I mean, okay, so Sean had a temper. But did he really try to kill somebody in a blind rage? Or was he just trying to scare me to make sure I wouldn't mess with Alyce?

I can't be sure, I decided. Sean is a friend. But still, I'd better be careful. Don't get him steamed.

I turned back to the others. "You guys look great," I told Raina and Joy. "What's up with you? What have you been up to since high school?"

"Going to college," Raina told me. "We're roommates at Duke."

Joy nodded. "Right, and we both have summer jobs waiting for us back in Shadyside. But they don't start for another week," she added with a grin. "So the two of us decided to have some fun."

"You definitely came to the right place," Ian told her. "The beach here is awesome."

"I still can't believe you're here too, Adam!" Joy exclaimed. "Did I tell you we were talking about you?"

Ian nudged me again. "Lucky you," he repeated.

I laughed. Joy always was a flirt, I remembered. "Yeah, you told me," I said to her. "What lies were you telling about me?"

Joy giggled.

Raina rolled her eyes. "Joy said she thought you were the biggest hunk in Shadyside High."

"Adam—a hunk?" Ian cried. "No way!"

"It's true," Joy told him. "And then he went and broke my heart," she added, pretending to pout.

"Me?" I raised my eyebrows. "I don't believe it. How did I break your heart?"

"By dumping me to go out with Raina," Joy declared.

"Excuse me?" Raina cried. "I didn't know Adam was seeing you before he asked me out!"

"Wait a sec!" I held up my hands. "I didn't dump you, Joy. We had exactly two dates, and then you fell madly in love with what's-his-name—Gary Brandt."

"Oh, him." Joy sighed. "He *was* awfully cute. But I wasn't in love with him. And I was *totally* devastated when you started going out with Raina," she added dramatically.

Raina rolled her eyes again. "Adam and I went to one movie together," she told Joy. "Right, Adam?"

"Right," I agreed. "And then we graduated and I got a job lifeguarding here before I went to college." I paused.

That was last summer, I thought. The summer I met Mitzi.

The summer Mitzi died.

"Adam?" Joy touched my arm again. "Are you okay? You look kind of serious all of a sudden."

"Yeah, did we say something wrong?" Raina asked. "We were just kidding around, you know."

"You didn't really break my heart," Joy admitted. Then she added. "Well, maybe a little."

"I still can't believe you're such a heartbreaker, buddy," Ian said, shaking his head. "Listen, I have to get back to work now. Catch you guys another time."

He gave a two-fingered salute to Joy and Raina, then trotted toward the boardwalk.

"Are you sure you're okay, Adam?" Joy asked again.

I took a deep breath. Don't think about Mitzi, I told myself. Joy and Raina are here to have fun. Why don't I give it a try too?

"I'm fine," I told them with a smile. "Really. Except I have to go on duty now and I'd rather hang out with you two."

"Well, we'll be here a whole week," Joy reminded me. "You don't work twenty-four hours a day, do you?"

"Nope. Hey, I know—let's have dinner in town tonight," I suggested. "There's this place on Main Street with great food and a live band. The Sea Shanty."

"Sounds perfect," Raina said.

"Great. Meet you there about seven." I smiled again, then began jogging across the beach toward the lifeguard station.

Sean waited on the platform, watching me. As I drew closer, he began climbing down the ladder. Must be in a real hurry, I thought. The head lifeguard would be really angry if he caught Sean leaving his post before I got there.

"Perfect timing, huh?" I called out as I trotted up. "I'm actually a minute early today."

Sean skipped the last few rungs and leapt down to the sand. He stood facing me, his dark eyes glaring angrily.

"Hey, what's your problem?" I asked. "What's wrong?"

He didn't answer. Just kept staring at me.

If looks could kill, I thought. "Hey, come on, man. What is it?"

Sean still didn't answer. The muscles in his arms tightened, and his jaw rippled as if he were grinding his teeth.

He took a step toward me and I tensed.

What is he going to do?

Chapter 13

"Sean—wh-what's wrong?" I stammered.

But he didn't answer.

Without uttering a word, he turned and ran off.

I watched for a second as he pounded across the sand. He's furious with me, I thought.

Be careful, I reminded myself. Sean is like a lit fuse. I don't want to be in the way when he blows.

As Sean disappeared into a crowd of sunbathers, I turned and climbed onto the platform. Settling in the lifeguard chair, I gazed out at the ocean.

Not too many swimmers in the water today. Not with the tide this high. But there were always a few who didn't care. Who liked to take chances.

I sighed, hoping nobody got into trouble.

A squeal of laughter from down the beach caught my attention. I glanced over.

Joy and Raina waded in the shallow water near the shore, gasping and shrieking whenever a tall wave crashed against their legs.

I smiled to myself. Having dinner with them would be fun. Joy would flirt and Raina would tease her, and we'd all laugh a lot.

And I wouldn't think about Mitzi.

For a short while, I'd forget.

The sun felt like fire on my head. I reached down to get my cap. And as I did, I spotted something blue and glittery bouncing up and down on the waves.

A water scooter.

I stood up and squinted.

At first the scooter was just a speck, but then it grew larger. And louder. I heard the buzz of the engine and saw the rider's knees bend as a strong wave slapped against his metallic blue machine.

The scooter kept coming, faster and faster. Getting closer to the shore.

Too close.

Was the guy an idiot? Didn't he know about the hidden rocks near the shoreline?

The dock had signs posted about how dangerous those rocks were. Everybody who took a scooter out got warned about them.

Couldn't the guy read? Didn't he listen?

The engine buzz grew louder.

The scooter roared over the tossing waves.

Closer. Closer to shore.

Moving in a fast, straight line.

The guy wasn't going to turn!

"No!" I shouted. I waved my arms and tried to get the guy's attention.

But the scooter kept coming. Aiming straight for the rocks.

I swung myself over the platform, clambered down the ladder, and raced toward the edge of the water.

"Turn!" I screamed over the noise of the engine. I waved both arms to one side. "Turn, turn!"

The scooter didn't turn. The guy stared straight ahead, but he didn't seem to see me at all.

I splashed into the water, shouting and waving my arms again. "You're going to crash!" I screamed. "Turn that thing! Turn it, turn it!"

The engine's buzz grew to a roar, and I ran farther out, until the waves slapped against my waist.

"Turn!" I screamed again, waving and motioning like crazy. "You're going to hit—"

I stopped suddenly, staring at the rider.

Hair flattened back against his head. Brown hair, exactly like mine.

A scattering of freckles across his slender shoulders. Like mine.

A blue nylon swimsuit with green stripes down the sides.

My suit.

My hair.

My face.

"It's me!" I gasped. "It's *me!*"

Chapter 14

"*I*t was me!" I declared to Dr. Thall that afternoon. "When I stared at the guy's face, it was like looking into a mirror. Except . . . none of it was real!"

Dr. Thall gazed at me from behind his desk, a thoughtful expression in his blue eyes. "Another hallucination," he murmured. "I'm glad you came to see me right away."

I nodded.

The whole thing had been a hallucination. No water scooter zooming toward the hidden rocks. No rider with my face, staring at me with my eyes.

None of it had happened.

Except for what *I* did, of course. Running into the ocean like a madman. Waving my arms at nothing. Screaming at a rider that didn't exist.

I shuddered, remembering how the people on the beach stared as I waded out of the water. At least Joy and Raina had been too far away to notice, I thought with relief.

But the others! The way they whispered to each other. The looks they gave me.

They thought I was a total wacko.

I raised my eyes to Dr. Thall. "Why does this keep happening?" I asked. "Am I really crazy?"

The doctor shook his head sharply. "I don't believe that for a minute, Adam. And I don't think you do either."

"I don't know what to think!" I told him. "I mean, why do I keep seeing things that aren't real? It's been a whole year since Mitzi died. You tell *me*, Doctor. If I'm not crazy, then what's going on?"

"The answer is still hidden," he replied. "That's what we have to work on, Adam. Something is still troubling you about Mitzi's accident. Something is still nagging at your mind and won't let go."

"But I thought we already worked all that out," I argued. "Mitzi died. I cracked up from guilt. I started seeing you. And now I realize it wasn't my fault. What else is there to work out?"

He shook his head. "Something hidden. Buried, deep down inside your mind. Something trying to work its way out. Something important."

He must be right, I thought with a sigh. Nothing else could explain the hallucinations.

But what was it?

As I thought hard about it, Dr. Thall rose from his chair. "Our time's up for today, Adam. But don't give up hope. We'll find out what's troubling you."

"How?" I demanded. "If it's buried so far down, how do we get it out? With dynamite?"

"Nothing as drastic as that," he assured me with a smile. "But there are still some experimental treatments we haven't tried."

"I'll try anything," I declared. "I have to find out what it is."

"Come on, Adam, let's dance!" Joy cried over the music blasting from the Sea Shanty's tiny stage. "I never did get a chance to dance with you in high school!"

"Neither did I," Raina told her. "But you went out with him two times. I dated him only once, so I should dance with him first."

"Whoa!" I said, laughing. "Don't I get to say anything about this?"

"Nope." Raina turned to Joy. "Let's flip for it," she suggested.

With a giggle, Joy fished around in her bag and finally pulled out a nickel. As she flipped it into the air, Raina called out heads.

We all watched as the coin spiraled halfway across the restaurant, landed on the floor, and skittered out of sight under a table.

Joy started to reach into her purse again, but I stopped her. "There's a simple solution to this problem," I announced, grabbing both their hands. "We all dance together."

As the band started a new number, the three of us squeezed our way through the tables and began to dance.

"I'm really glad you invited us, Adam!" Joy

shouted, her brown curls bouncing. "I'm having a great time."

"Me too," I told her. And I was. Not that I'd forgotten my hallucination that morning. I couldn't.

But with Joy and Raina around, I could shove it to the back of my mind.

I'd felt so low after I'd left Dr. Thall, I thought about canceling the dinner.

I'm glad I didn't, I thought as I spun around and faced Raina. This is more fun than sitting in the apartment, worrying about going nuts.

I'd had a good time last night too, but this was better. Raina and Joy were old friends. And they really liked to laugh and goof around.

Dr. Thall said he wanted to try some experimental treatments. Fine. In the meantime, I decided to have as much fun as I could.

As I turned back to dance with Joy, I spotted Ian. He sat at a table way across the room. I waved, but he didn't notice.

Maybe I should go over there, I thought. Ask him to eat with us.

Then Ian leaned his elbows on the table and said something, and I saw that he wasn't alone. Across the table from him sat a girl with long black hair and a great tan.

No wonder he didn't notice me, I thought with a grin. And he wouldn't want to join the three of us either. He's too busy trying to impress his latest date.

"Hey, our food's ready!" Raina called out, pointing toward the table. "Let's eat."

We hurried back and sat down. The waiter set out bowls of corn-on-the-cob and salad, then dumped three boiled crabs onto the paper-covered table.

With bibs around our necks, we cracked the crabs and began dipping the meat into melted butter. As I reached for a piece of corn, I suddenly saw her.

Leslie.

She stood inside the doorway, staring across the crowded dining room, straight at me.

She wore a yellow sundress that showed off her tan, and her dark hair gleamed under the lights. She looked fantastic.

But her eyes flashed with anger.

Oh, great, I thought unhappily. She thinks I'm sneaking around on her or something. She doesn't know Joy and Raina are just good friends.

When Leslie saw me staring at her, she pushed away from the door and began striding toward our table.

She's going to make a big scene, I thought. Stop her.

I shoved my chair back and stood up, yanking the paper bib off.

"Hey, as long as you're up, could you find the waiter and order me another ginger ale?" Raina asked.

"Sure." I dropped the bib on the table and turned to go, but Joy grabbed my arm. "Me too," she said.

"Huh?" What was she talking about?

"A ginger ale," Joy repeated. "I'd like another one too, please."

"Right. Two ginger ales." I gave them a quick smile and started to hurry away.

But my foot caught on the leg of my chair. And by the time I got myself untangled, Leslie had reached the table.

"Leslie, hi. I . . . uh, didn't expect to see you here," I stammered.

She crossed her arms, her gray eyes flashing again.

73

"I'll just bet you didn't. Looks like you're having a great time," she added bitterly, glancing at Joy and Raina.

"Listen, Leslie—" I began to say.

"Even better than last night, right?" she interrupted. "I mean, this time you're out with *two* new friends."

"Huh? What's that supposed to mean?"

"I saw you out last night, Adam," Leslie declared. "You told me you felt lousy and you were going to lie down, remember? So I decided to take a walk. And guess who I saw, strolling along Main Street with another girl?"

"I'm sorry," I told her. "I really am, Leslie. That girl—I met her on the beach and we just kind of decided to go out. It's not a major romance or anything."

"Oh, gee, I *really* feel a lot better now," she said sarcastically.

"Leslie, I'm sorry," I repeated. "It just happened. I didn't mean to hurt you."

"Forget it," she snapped, glaring at Joy and Raina. "I can see you're busy anyway."

"Hey, come on," I pleaded. "Joy and Raina are friends from high school."

"So what?" she demanded. "You're out with them instead of me. And you lied to me about last night. How do you think that makes me feel?"

Before I could think of anything to say, Leslie grabbed my arm and shoved me backward against the table.

Joy and Raina gasped, and I heard a plate crash to the floor.

"You hurt me, Adam!" she declared furiously. "And I'm going to find a way to hurt you back!"

"Huh? What are you *saying?* You—you don't mean that!" I cried.

Without another word, Leslie turned and stormed away from the table.

"Leslie—stop! You don't mean that!" I called after her. "You don't!"

Chapter 15

The next day, I hurried to get to my lifeguard post on time. "Don't bother to come up, Adam," Sean said, staring down at me from the platform.

"Why not?" I stopped, one foot on the ladder, and squinted up at him. "Don't tell me I'm early," I joked.

Sean's lips curved—in a sneer, not a smile.

So much for hoping he'd be in a better mood today. "Why shouldn't I come up?" I repeated. "The tide is getting high—somebody needs to put out the warning flags."

"No kidding." He turned away for a few seconds, then turned back, one hand clutching the red flags. "Here. You take care of it."

Aiming one of the flags like a spear, he sailed it over the edge of the platform. It stuck in the sand, wobbled, and then fell.

As I bent to pick it up, another one stabbed the ground inches from my feet.

"Hey!" I shouted. "Watch it—will you?"

"Oops. My aim must be off," Sean replied. He drew his arm back and pitched the last flag straight out toward the shoreline. "How's that?"

"Just great," I muttered, frowning up at him. "Thanks a lot."

Sean gazed back, a cold expression on his face. "Better take care of those flags," he told me. "Tide's rising, remember?" Without another word he turned away and sat down in his chair.

I stood there a few seconds, furious. Go up and confront him, I told myself. Tell him he's acting like a total jerk.

Right, and get pounded to a pulp. At least wait until he's cooled down a little.

Pushing the anger away, I picked up the two flags, then set off toward the water. As I did, I spotted Raina and Joy waving to me from under a pink-and-green-striped beach umbrella.

Great, I thought. All they probably want to talk about is the ugly scene with Leslie last night at dinner.

All *I* wanted to do was forget it.

"Adam!" Joy shouted. She stood up and waved her arms. "Hi, Adam!"

I waved back, then sighed. Might as well get it over with, I decided.

I worked my way to their umbrella, sticking one of the flags in the sand as I went. When I strode up, they exchanged a glance, then grinned at me. "I'm so relieved!" Joy exclaimed dramatically. "I mean, you're still alive!"

"Yeah, we were afraid Leslie might have mugged

you on your way home or something," Raina agreed. She tsk-tsked. "See what happens when you cheat on your girlfriend, Adam?"

"You'd better be real careful with your mail," Joy added. "She might decide to send you a really dynamite package." She fluffed up her brown hair and giggled. *"Dynamite—get it?"*

"Yeah, I get it," I told her. "Listen, I hurt Leslie's feelings. I don't blame her for being steamed."

"Well, *I* don't either," Joy told me. "But she was more than steamed—she was ballistic!"

The blazing look in Leslie's eyes flashed into my mind. And I heard her words again—*You hurt me, Adam. I'm going to find a way to hurt you back.*

Is Joy right? I wondered. Did Leslie really mean it?

Of course not, I decided. People say dumb things when they're angry.

Shaking away the memory, I began to work a flag into the sand. "I'm sorry about last night," I told them. "But I don't feel like joking about it, okay?"

"Okay. Sorry." Raina exchanged another quick glance with Joy, then reached into her beach bag and took out a tube of sunscreen. "What's the flag for?" she asked, rubbing some lotion on her arms.

"High tide," I explained. "There's probably a strong undercurrent."

"We can still go swimming, can't we?" Joy asked anxiously.

"Yeah, if you really want to," I told her. "But what's the rush?"

"No rush. We're just dying to get in the water, that's all," Raina told me quickly. "I mean, we're not going to be here all summer or anything."

"Well, go ahead," I said. "Just stay close to shore

and be careful." I left them and walked farther down the beach to post the last flag.

Heading back toward the lifeguard station, I saw them in the water, splashing each other and laughing. The waves didn't come any higher than their knees, so I knew they'd be okay.

When I climbed onto the platform, Sean gave me a quick glance, his eyes narrowed to slits. Then he turned his gaze back to the ocean.

Definitely not in a better mood, I decided.

Stepping over his feet, I climbed into my chair and checked out the beach. On the right, a bunch of little kids built a sand castle, digging a moat and letting the waves fill it up.

Farther down, an old couple walked slowly, their heads bent as they searched for shells.

A group of noisy high school kids played keep-away with a Frisbee.

Plenty of people were in the water, but most of them stayed close to shore. I spotted Joy in her bright pink swimsuit and Raina in a black one. They were still only knee-deep.

Everything seemed under control.

I turned to Sean.

He sat like a statue, his face straight ahead. Only his eyes moved, swiveling back and forth as he kept watch on the crowd.

Shrugging, I reached into my bag and pulled out a bottle of water. I tilted my head back for a drink—and heard a high, shrill scream.

"Huh?"

I leapt to my feet, my heart pounding in fear, my eyes scanning the water and the beach.

Another scream. A flash of red to my right.

79

"It's mine!" a little girl shrieked as she tried to yank a red pail away from another little kid. "Let go, you dummy, it's mine!"

Her voice spiraled up and up, into another ear-splitting scream.

The other little kid finally let go. The girl plopped into the sand and immediately stopped screaming.

I shook my head. Get a grip, I told myself. It was just a battle over a plastic pail.

Nobody's in trouble.

I stretched my arms and scanned the beach again.

And then I saw Joy and Raina.

Waving to me from far out in the water.

Too far out.

Why did they go out so far? I wondered.

Did the undertow pull them? Are they in trouble?

Raina's blond head disappeared for a moment. Then it bobbed up again. The two of them frantically waved their arms over their heads.

My heart raced.

The current is carrying them farther and farther out, I realized. They *are* in trouble!

Another wave swelled, covering both girls completely.

This time neither one of them came up.

Chapter 16

*T*his isn't happening. It can't be real! I told myself. It's another hallucination!

I told them to stay close to shore. They're not stupid. They wouldn't take chances.

It *has* to be another hallucination. I'm seeing things again.

I squeezed my eyes shut, then snapped them open.

Both girls had surfaced. I could see them clearly, bobbing up and down in the water.

But they were still too far out.

And still waving frantically.

I squinted to see better.

Raina had tilted her head back, trying to keep her mouth and nose above water.

Joy stared straight ahead, slapping the water wildly. Thrashing and kicking.

Out of control.

Both girls had lost control.

The current was carrying them away.

I blinked again. Stared hard.

Joy had disappeared.

But I could still see Raina, waving and thrashing. Her face was a pale smudge on the dark water. Her mouth was open in a desperate scream.

It's really happening! I realized to my horror.

It's real!

"Let's go!" I shouted, shoving away from the railing. "Come on, Sean, we—"

I broke off, stunned.

Sean's chair was empty.

He's already on his way, I thought as I hurried toward the ladder.

But then I noticed the life preserver. Still in its place.

And Sean's duffel bag was gone.

He left. He left to take his break without telling me. I'm on my own.

Grabbing the life preserver and the rope, I pitched them over the platform, then clambered down the ladder.

I picked up the preserver and charged down the beach. As I raced across the sand, I grabbed my whistle and gave it several piercing blasts. Maybe the head lifeguard would hear me from his office on the boardwalk.

People scattered in front of me. The little girl with the red bucket shrieked again. The high school kids dived out of my way as I pounded toward the water.

I blew the whistle again. Maybe Sean will hear it, I thought desperately. Maybe he didn't go very far and he'll hear the whistle and come back to help.

At the water's edge I paused and stared out at the ocean, gasping for breath.

I couldn't see Joy and Raina at all.

Had the current pulled them under?

I glanced back and forth.

No sign of Sean.

He didn't hear me, I realized. He's not coming.

Everyone else on the beach stood frozen, staring out at the water.

Watching. Waiting. Wondering what was happening. All over.

"There!" a guy shouted hoarsely. "I see something over there!"

My gaze snapped to where he pointed.

At first I saw only waves. Frothy, churning, sounding like thunder as they rolled in.

But then I saw the hands.

Two hands above the water, the fingers stretched up to the sky.

Slowly, they sank beneath the surface.

Only *two* hands? I thought as I dashed along the wet, hard-packed sand. Joy's? Raina's?

Had one of them already drowned? Would I be too late?

No! Don't even think it! I told myself.

Get out there and get them!

I slung the life preserver over one shoulder and raced into the water.

Sucking in a deep breath, I plunged under the first wave and began swimming toward Joy and Raina.

I'll find them! I vowed as I struggled through the waves. I'll be there in less than a minute.

But then a question flashed into my mind. A question that nearly paralyzed me in fear.

Once I'm out there, how will I do it?

How can I save them both?

Chapter 17

I broke the surface, gasping.

Before I could catch my breath, another towering wave broke over me and I went under again.

I could feel the current tugging at me, tugging me hard, tugging me farther out. Fighting against it, I rose to the surface with another choking gasp.

I swiped the water from my eyes and mouth, then squinted against the glare.

No hands reached above the water now. All I saw was churning white foam.

Was I too late?

Another powerful wave washed over me, and I went under. The strong undertow dragged at me. My ears filled with a dull, roaring sound.

I fought my way up, struggling hard not to lose the

life preserver. Saltwater stung my eyes and blurred my vision.

I shook my head and blinked furiously.

Where were they?

Where?

Water sloshed into my mouth. Spitting it out, I sucked in a deep breath of air and screamed as loud as I could. "Joy! Raina!"

More water washed into my mouth and nose. Sputtering and choking, I screamed their names again. Then I kicked hard and began to swim.

After a few more strokes I pulled up and scanned the rolling water.

There!

Somebody's head, just above the surface.

Eyes wide in terror.

Joy!

Another head bobbed up, blond hair streaming with water. I caught a quick glimpse of Raina's panic-filled eyes, and then she sank again.

But they're both there! I thought. They're still alive!

Adrenaline surged through me, and I plunged forward, my arms pumping furiously.

Above the ocean's roar I heard another sound. No words. Just a high-pitched scream of horror.

Probably Joy. Raina looked too weak to scream.

"Hang on!" I urged them as I swam. "Hang on!"

I drew up again—and saw Joy only a few feet away from me.

Raina was nowhere in sight.

I sucked in as much air as I could, then launched myself through the water toward Joy.

When I was only a couple of strokes from her, Raina's head bobbed up in front of me.

She looks dead, I thought. Blank eyes. Waxy skin. She's not even struggling anymore.

As Raina began to sink again, I dived under, grabbed her around the waist with one arm, and pulled—pulled—pulled her to the surface.

"Okay, I've got you!" I gasped, struggling to hold her head above the swirling waves. "I've got you!"

Raina didn't respond. Her head lolled to the side. Her slippery body hung limply, its weight pulling us both down.

I kicked hard and yanked her up again. Was she breathing? I couldn't tell.

"Hang on, hang on!" I muttered as I struggled to get her into the life preserver. "Come on, Raina! Help yourself! Don't give up now!"

Raina still didn't respond.

A wave rolled over us. The water pushed, then pulled. Raina almost slipped out of my grasp. But I snagged the strap of her swimsuit and dragged her closer to me.

Only a few seconds before another wave hits, I thought. Then another, and another.

Get the life preserver on her!

Breathing harshly, I finally managed to wrestle Raina into the life preserver.

And then something landed heavily on my back.

Fingers dug into my shoulders.

An arm wrapped around my neck, tightening like a vise.

And Joy's shriek of panic sounded in my ear.

"Help! Help me, Adam!" She gulped and coughed as water surged into her mouth. "Help me!"

Her arm pressed hard against my throat, choking

me. Keeping the preserver's rope in one hand, I grabbed Joy's arm with the other and pulled it loose.

"Let go!" I shouted. "I'll help you—but you have to let go!"

Her scream rose again. Piercing. Hysterical.

She grabbed hold of my head with both hands. Her fingers clutched at my hair and stabbed me in the eye.

Another powerful wave pitched against us.

Raina's body bumped me. And as we broke the surface, she rolled onto her stomach, her face in the water.

I yanked hard on the rope. Joy's nails bit painfully into my face. She pushed on my head, struggling to lift herself higher and higher.

I sank down, then kicked my way back up, sputtering and trying to throw Joy off me. "Let go!" I screamed. "Joy! Let go!"

Another wave loosened Joy's hold on me and brought Raina closer. I grabbed Raina's shoulder and rolled her over so she faced the sky.

I still couldn't tell if she was breathing.

But she might be, I told myself. I can't give up on her.

Got to get her to shore—fast.

Before I could move, Joy leapt onto my back again, crying and screaming. Totally panicked. Out of control.

"Joy!" I shouted as I fought to keep her from pulling me under. "Raina's in bad shape. I need your help!"

Joy didn't hear me. Her hands gripped my shoulders. Her legs wrapped around me as if I were giving her a piggyback ride.

Still screaming wildly, she tried to climb up my back and onto my shoulders.

My head quickly went under, and I swallowed a mouthful of water. Joy clung to me, struggling, screaming, her weight pushing me farther and farther down.

Desperate for air, I twisted sideways and kicked hard. Joy rolled off my back, still clutching one of my arms. Kicking again, I fought my way to the surface.

My chest ached as I gasped in some air. "Joy, listen to me!" I shouted hoarsely. "Try to calm down! You're okay, but Raina isn't! She needs your help, Joy! *I* need it!"

Her eyes wild with panic, Joy choked and sputtered and clawed at my arms. Then she began screaming again.

"Joy!" I shouted into her face. "Stop fighting! Help me!"

Joy clung to me, still screaming.

I glanced at Raina, floating so limply, so lifelessly, in the water.

Joy's grip tightened. We started to sink again.

She'll pull us all down, I thought. Do something!

I can't rescue them both, I realized. I have to make a choice.

Decide!

"Joy!" I shouted. "Raina might be dying. I have to get her to shore!"

It's your only choice, I thought. Save Raina. Then get Joy.

"Stay here, Joy!" I screamed. "You're fine. You're not hurt! I'll take Raina in and come back for you!"

With a wordless cry, Joy plunged forward and slung her arms around my neck.

"Get off, Joy!" I screamed. "Get off and I'll come back for you!"

My head went under again. I tried to kick my way up, but Joy's weight dragged me deeper and deeper. As I fought to shove her off, she grabbed the rope and pulled Raina under too.

Wave after wave surged over us.

The current pulled and tugged, taking us farther from shore.

My heart thundered in my chest and ears.

My lungs screamed for air.

I kicked again, stretched my neck, tried to get my head above water.

But I couldn't break the surface.

The three of us sank down, farther and farther.

The weight of the water pressed on my ears, pounded against my head.

I'm getting weaker, I thought.

My strength is giving out.

And time is running out.

All three of us are going to drown.

All three of us . . .

Chapter 18

My lungs were on fire. My chest felt ready to burst.

I clamped my jaw tight, fighting against the urge to open my mouth.

If I breathed now, I'd die.

We'd all die.

But I couldn't hold out much longer. Only seconds, and I'd have to give in and breathe.

One of Joy's arms slipped away from my neck. As she struggled to catch hold again, I grabbed her wrist.

Then I kicked hard, again and again, trying desperately to kick my way to the top.

Keep going, Adam! I ordered myself. Keep kicking! Don't give up now!

Don't give up. . . .

Joy's weight dragged at me, but I could see the

sunlight on the surface of the water now. No way would I shut my eyes and let us sink down into the dark.

I gave another desperate kick. This time my head shot out of the water.

Exhausted, I gulped in breath after breath of air. My legs felt so heavy, heavy as lead.

My head pounded and my chest still burned. If only I could just lie back and float.

Beside me, Joy choked and coughed and tried to grab me in another stranglehold.

Save Raina, I told myself. Get her to shore.

Then come back and get Joy.

Then I can rest.

Before Joy could clamp her arms around me again, I shoved her away. "Stop fighting!" I cried. "Stop fighting and you'll be okay!"

"Nooo!" Joy reached out frantically, thrashed her arms, tried to grab my head.

I batted her hands away and paddled backward. "I'll come back for you, Joy!" I promised. "All you have to do is hold on!"

Joy shook her head, gasping hysterically and reaching out for me again. "Please!" she begged. "Don't let me drown! Please!"

"You won't!" I dragged Raina close to my side and got one arm around her. "You won't drown—I won't let you! Listen to me—I'll come right back!"

"Nooo!" Joy cried, thrashing toward me through the water. "Adam, please don't leave me! Take us both! Please—don't let me drown!"

"I won't!" I shouted. With one arm around Raina, I kicked away and began swimming toward the shore. "I'll come back for you, Joy! I promise!"

I stroked hard with my free arm, swallowing water, choking, dragging Raina along.

Behind me, Joy's terrified screams filled the air.

I shuddered with guilt.

But I kept swimming away from her.

I did the right thing, I told myself. I couldn't save them both at once.

"Adaaaam!" Joy's cry sounded farther away now.

And weaker.

Don't look back, I thought. Don't stop. Joy can still scream, and that's good. She'll be okay. Get Raina out first, then go back.

My legs grew even heavier as I struggled against the current. My arms felt ready to fall off.

Water kept sloshing into my mouth, and my breath came in raspy, choking gasps.

I can't make it, I thought. I'm not strong enough.

I pulled harder. Kicking . . . kicking . . .

I tried to kick away my discouraging thoughts. Kick the ache from my muscles. Kick . . . kick . . . kick so hard I wouldn't feel the ache, or the burning in my chest . . .

Keep going, I ordered myself. Don't give up.

If I give up, we'll all die.

Trying to keep Raina's head from sinking, I dragged my arm through the water again. Kicked my legs. Stroked. Kicked.

Stroke. Kick.

One more stroke, and my fingers scraped against the sandy bottom.

Almost out! Almost safe!

I rested my knees on the sand, then slowly rose to my feet. My arms shook with exhaustion. My legs felt like jelly.

Got to go back for Joy, I thought. Pull Raina out, then go back.

Bending over, I got both arms under Raina's shoulders and dragged her through the last few feet of water.

Gasping for breath, I collapsed beside her. Started to turn her over.

I heard shouts and cries. People running toward us.

Raina's back suddenly heaved. I heard a choking sound, and then water spewed from her mouth.

She's alive! I saw. She'll make it.

Got to get Joy now, I told myself. Raina's okay. Got to go back for Joy, as I promised.

Sucking in a deep breath, I pushed myself to my feet and turned back to the ocean.

Joy?

No head bobbed above the water now. No hands stretched up. No screams filled the air.

Joy? Where are you?

I squinted into the tossing waves.

Joy?

Joy had disappeared beneath the waves.

I was too late.

PART THREE

Chapter 19

ADAM

Someone groaned.

Raina?

I turned to look, but I couldn't see her. I couldn't see anything. Everything had gone totally dark.

The groan came again. Louder this time.

I'm groaning, I realized. I'm the one who is groaning.

I turned back the other way. Something soft and heavy hit my face.

I reached over to shove it away.

And woke up, clutching a pillow in my hand.

My pillow, I realized, as I gazed around the room. I'm in my bed. My apartment.

I sat up, confused. "What . . . happened?"

Ian entered the bedroom. "You *are* awake," he said. "I thought I heard you stirring. How do you feel?"

"Ian!" I cried. My throat still burned. I felt so weak.

"Ian—was it a hallucination?" I choked out. "Please—tell me that it didn't happen. Tell me that Joy didn't drown."

Ian lowered his head. "I'm sorry, Adam," he said softly.

"Sorry?" I cried, hopelessly confused. The room tilted. I felt as if I might tumble out of bed. "Sorry? What do you mean? Was it real, Ian? Or did I imagine it?"

Ian bit his lower lip. "You didn't imagine it," he replied grimly.

I gasped.

"The head lifeguard brought you home, Adam. The doctor was here. He just left a few minutes ago."

"I—I don't remember any of that," I stammered.

I grabbed the bed sheet tightly, so tightly my hands ached. I could still feel the tossing currents, the hard, cold slap of the waves. The whole room rocked and tossed.

"Please, Ian," I begged. "Tell me it was just another crazy hallucination."

He sat down on the edge of the bed. "I wish I could. I wish I could tell you that everything was okay, Adam. But—" His voice cracked.

"But your friend drowned," he continued, avoiding my stare. "You did your best. Everyone on the beach saw you. Everyone said you did what you had to do."

"But—Joy drowned?" I whispered.

Ian nodded.

I've killed another girl!

The horrifying thought burst into my head.

Another one . . . I've killed another one.

"You saved one," Ian said softly. "You can feel

good about that, Adam. You saved one. And you saved yourself."

"I wish I had drowned!" I screamed.

"No. Come on, man," Ian said. "Don't say that. You were really brave. That's what the head lifeguard said. That's what everyone said. You had to do it all on your own, since Sean left you there."

I fell back on my pillow. I felt so weak. So totally exhausted. I couldn't talk anymore.

"You okay?" Ian asked. "Should I call the doctor back?"

"No need," I muttered.

I shut my eyes and saw Joy again.

Mitzi and Joy. Joy and Mitzi.

Ian stood up and crossed the room. He picked up the phone.

"Who are you calling?" I asked, my voice hoarse.

"I have a date," Ian replied. "I'm going to call her and cancel it so I can stay home with you." He started punching numbers on the dial.

"No. Don't cancel it," I said. "Go ahead. Go out. I'm just going to sleep. I—I can't really talk anyway."

Ian hesitated, the receiver in his hand. "You sure? You sure you'll be okay?"

I sighed. "I need to be by myself," I told him.

Ian set the phone down. Then he made his way to the closet and pulled out a black and green windbreaker. "The wind's whipping up out there," he told me, shrugging into the jacket. "And a bunch of mean-looking clouds are rolling in."

I pictured the clouds over the ocean. Dark. Mean-looking, like Ian said. With the wind up, the water would turn mean too. Rough and choppy.

And Joy's body was somewhere out there.

Would she wash up onshore?

Or was she gone for good, buried under tons of water?

I shuddered, then raised my eyes to Ian. "Is that my new windbreaker?"

"Yeah." He grinned sheepishly. "You don't mind if I borrow it, do you?"

I started to say yes, then changed my mind. What did I care if he wore it? What difference did it make? "Go ahead," I told him.

"Thanks. Hey, I'll even hang it up when I get back."

"Huh?" I felt dazed. Shattered. I couldn't even hear him. I still had the roar of the ocean waves in my ears.

And Joy's frantic cries . . .

Ian started to zip the jacket, then stopped. "Are you sure you don't want me to hang around? It's no big deal to break the date. We could watch the tube or play cards or something. You know. To take your mind off what happened."

"No, you go on," I insisted.

"What are you going to do?" he asked. "Are you really going to sleep? Do you think you should call Dr. Thall?"

"Too many questions," I groaned, rubbing my head. I sank back into the pillow. "Too many questions . . ."

"Well, take care of yourself," Ian said. "I'll call you later. You know. Just to see how you're doing."

He paused at the door and turned back to me. "I'm real sorry, Adam. After last summer, you deserve a break. You really do."

I didn't know what to say. So I stared up at the ceiling, wishing the bed would stop tossing and heaving.

The front door slammed.

The refrigerator hummed, then kicked off.

The apartment grew quiet.

Outside, I could hear the dull roar of the waves. Breaking against the shore. Falling back. Then rushing in again.

Over and over.

Joy's out there, I thought.

The ocean is tossing her around like a piece of seaweed.

What does she look like now? Are her eyes still wide and filled with terror? Is her mouth still open in a soundless scream?

As I squeezed my eyes shut against the image, I heard Joy's voice again, pleading with me not to leave her. I shook my head and clamped my hands over my ears.

But I still saw the image of her horrified face.

And I still felt the horrible guilt.

With a gasp, I swung my feet to the floor and stood up. Do something, I thought. Don't keep sitting around thinking about things. If you do, you'll definitely freak out.

Go for a walk? Maybe later, I thought. I still felt wiped out.

If only I could sleep. But if I slept, I knew I'd dream. And the last thing I wanted was another nightmare.

I went into the living room and slipped a CD on. The throbbing bass of the rock band filled the apartment, shutting out the sound of the ocean.

My stomach rumbled, so I fixed a bowl of cereal.

Okay, I told myself, I'll eat, thumb through some magazines, listen to the music.

Anything to keep Joy out of my mind.

Anything to stop feeling guilty.

As I started to sit on the couch, the bowl of cereal tilted, sloshing cold milk and soggy cornflakes down the front of my T-shirt.

I set the dripping bowl on the coffee table, then quickly pulled the shirt off. Time to change anyway, I thought with a shiver. Air's getting colder.

Back in the bedroom, I pulled on a pair of jeans, then rummaged through a drawer for a sweatshirt. As I straightened up, I caught a glimpse of myself in the mirror.

My eyes stared back.

I quickly turned away. I couldn't stand to look at myself.

You killed Joy, my eyes were accusing me.

But I couldn't save them both! I argued.

I took a deep breath, trying to calm myself.

And the phone rang.

I stumbled to the table and picked it up. "Hello?" I answered shakily.

"Adam," a voice whispered. The whisper was so low, so hoarse, I couldn't tell if it was a boy or girl.

"Adam, you're going to pay for what you did to me. I promise you. You're going to pay soon."

Chapter 20

My heart stuttered, then began pounding as hard as before. I tried to speak, but my throat closed up.

"You're going to pay for what you did to me." The hoarse whisper sounded like an ocean wave, breaking in my ear.

"Who . . ." I choked out. "Who is this?"

A click.

Then a dial tone.

I slammed the phone down, then stared at it tensely.

Would it ring again?

Who was it? Who had a grudge against me?

Sean does, I thought.

And Leslie is furious with me. She said she'd find a way to pay me back. I didn't think she meant it.

But maybe she did.

Or maybe the call was just a prank.

In the living room, the CD ended. The apartment grew quiet again.

The phone didn't ring.

My heart still jumped around in my chest. My palms felt sweaty, and my foot tapped nervously on the floor.

Get out, I thought. Get out of the apartment and walk until your mind is a total blank.

Yanking the sweatshirt down over my head, I put on my sneakers and hurried out of the apartment.

Outside, I took off in a fast jog, running across the road and scrambling over the dunes. My legs ached from kicking so hard, so desperately in the ocean. But I didn't care.

I just wanted to run and run. Run away from myself . . .

After a few moments I stopped, staring up and down the empty beach.

I could hear the waves rolling in and out, but I couldn't see them.

Thick fog blanketed everything. It rolled along the sand and swirled around me like billowing smoke.

Cold. Wet. Eerie.

Maybe I should go back, I thought. The beach feels so creepy with all this fog.

No, I decided. Walking around is better than being inside.

Walk. Don't go back until you're so tired, you'll sleep without dreaming.

I trotted closer to the shoreline, then began to walk down the beach along the firm, wet sand.

The fog seemed to grow thicker, blanketing me like

wet cotton. Except for the sound of the waves and a distant foghorn, I heard nothing.

And saw no one.

Every time I thought of Joy and Mitzi, or heard that hoarse, whispered voice in my head, I picked up my pace. Grabbed a piece of driftwood and tossed it into the waves. Ran until my legs ached even harder.

Anything to keep from thinking about what had happened that afternoon. The horrible choice I had to make . . .

As I ran, an outcropping of dark, jagged rocks suddenly appeared through the fog, only a few feet in front of me. Waves crashed against them, splashing and churning.

I stopped, winded and exhausted. And my mind felt as tired as my legs, I realized. Good time to go back. Just hit the bed and sleep.

I pressed my hands on my thighs and bent over for a few seconds to catch my breath.

When I straightened up, a figure stepped out from behind the rocks.

"Hi," I called out, peering through the fog. "I thought I was the only one on the beach tonight."

The figure moved a step closer. Didn't speak.

"Hi," I repeated.

A gust of wind came up. The fog swirled and lifted for a moment.

And I saw that it was a girl. Barefoot.

I squinted hard, trying to see her face.

But it was hidden in the thick fog.

She stepped closer. She moved silently, as if floating, floating with the swirling fog curtain.

Why did I suddenly feel so cold?

Her windbreaker flew up behind her, like a cape. In the dark mist, she looked almost transparent. As if she were part of the shadows, part of the fog. As if I could see right through her.

I took a step back, suddenly chilled.

Suddenly afraid.

If only I could see her face.

The dark windbreaker billowed in the wind. Wisps of fog appeared to circle her.

"Adam . . ." she whispered.

I gasped. She knew my name!

"Adam—you let me drown!"

"NOOO!" I cried.

Joy! It was Joy floating in the shadows, billowing in the fog.

Joy's ghost, come back to haunt me.

I took a deep breath. "You're not real!" I cried.

A wave crashed close beside me. My skin dripped from the icy ocean spray.

She took another step toward me, her bare feet so silent, silent as a ghost.

"You're not Joy!" I cried, my voice muffled by the fog. By my fear. "You're not real. I'm imagining you. And you're going to go away now!"

"Adam . . ." she whispered. *"Adam . . ."*

I felt a chill. Then another. I realized my whole body was shaking.

Don't run, I ordered myself, squeezing my eyes shut. Don't freak out. When you open your eyes, she'll be gone.

Because she's not here. She's not real!

Joy is dead.

Slowly, I opened my eyes.

In front of me, the fog began to move.

I held my breath as it swirled and lifted.

Revealing nothing.

No one.

"I knew it!" I cried out loud.

I knew she wasn't real!

Almost laughing, I raised both arms above my head, as if I'd just won a fight. I *did* win a fight, I thought. I didn't let the hallucination fool me this time.

I fought it away.

Feeling a little better, I dropped my arms and stuck my hands in my pockets.

And gasped as I saw the footprints.

Footprints of bare feet in the sand. Facing me.

Exactly where Joy had stood.

I stood there, shivering. My heart pounding. My head throbbing.

Stood and stared at the footprints in the sand.

And wondered: Since when do hallucinations leave footprints?

Chapter 21

I slammed the apartment door shut and leaned against it, breathless from the run home.

And from fear.

Joy *did* appear in front of you tonight, I told myself for the thousandth time.

But she's dead. Isn't she?

And the footprints?

The footprints . . .

I couldn't explain it. I couldn't understand it. I knew only that the footprints were real.

And the girl whispering to me through the fog was real. Not a hallucination.

I couldn't see her face. The fog and the shadows kept that from me.

But I saw her bathing suit. Joy's bathing suit. And I heard her voice, so weak, so faint.

"Adam, you let me drown. . . ."

Joy. Joy's ghost.

A low, rumbling noise made me jump. Gasping, I glanced tensely around the empty living room.

"Who's here?" I called, craning my neck as I tried to see into the bedroom. "Ian?"

No answer.

"Ian? Are you back?"

The rumbling rose to a steady, low-pitched hum.

The refrigerator, I realized, shaking my head in disgust. What is *wrong* with me? I'm terrified by the refrigerator!

You're really losing it, Adam, I scolded myself. And you're totally wiped out. Go to bed. Don't think anymore. Don't try to figure things out.

Just get some sleep.

The instant I thought about sleep, a wave of exhaustion washed over me.

My eyelids drooped heavily as I crossed the living room. I bumped into the coffee table, sloshing more milk out of the cereal bowl I'd left there earlier.

I stopped. Yawned. Don't be a slob, I told myself. At least put the bowl in the sink.

But the thought of lifting a bowl and walking a few extra steps made me even more tired. Almost dizzy, I stumbled my way into the bedroom.

Collapsing across the bed, I closed my eyes and fell into a deep sleep.

I tossed my head back and forth on the pillow, trying to escape the dream.

I'm having a dream, I told myself. I can feel the blanket under my face. The damp clamminess of my sweatshirt and jeans.

I was sprawled across my bed. I hadn't even bothered to get undressed. And I was dreaming again. And I knew it.

Snap out of it, I thought. Wake up!

But I couldn't do it. The dream pulled me further and further in, until I couldn't feel the blanket or the wet clothes any longer.

Instead, I felt the hot sun on my head and the water lapping at my legs as I waded into the ocean.

Wind swept across the water, flinging the salt spray higher and higher. Gulls shrieked as the gusts blew them sideways. The waves rolled and churned, crashing toward the shore.

I dove under, surfaced, and swam farther out until the sandy bottom dropped away.

As I pulled up and began to tread water, a speck of color caught my eye.

A speck of bright electric blue, rocking across the waves.

The water scooter.

The speck grew larger as the scooter came closer to me. The sound of its engine buzzed in my brain.

My heart began to pound.

Would it crash on the hidden rocks?

The engine roared, then began to fade as the scooter turned sharply and headed back out.

Too far out, I thought.

The water's too rough. The waves will toss that thing around like a toy boat and break it to pieces.

I started to swim again, keeping my eye on the scooter. Maybe I could wave it down, get it to stop.

As I fought my way through the waves, the scooter turned again. Started coming back toward me.

Two people rode it. A guy and a girl.

I squinted against the glare, trying to see their faces. Who were they?

The scooter bumped and rocked, getting closer.

I could see the girl's face now. Laughing. Tossing her head and laughing as the water scooter leapt into the air.

Joy's face.

As the scooter cut into a sharp turn, the girl laughed and tossed her head again.

And her long blond hair whipped out behind her.

Not Joy, I thought.

Mitzi!

But who's the guy? It's supposed to be me, but I'm already in the water, watching.

So who's riding the water scooter with Mitzi?

As I stared, the scooter leapt over another wave, rose into the air, and slapped down hard. A second wave rose up, tossing the scooter sideways.

Tossing Mitzi into the water.

No! I thought, my heart pounding harder. It's happening again!

The water scooter spun around. Picked up speed as it aimed straight for Mitzi.

Stop! I wanted to yell. Can't you see her? She's right in front of you. Turn back!

But the words seemed trapped inside me.

And the water scooter kept zooming across the water, roaring closer and closer to Mitzi.

My eyes burned as I strained to see better. Who's the guy on it? Why can't I see his face?

Who is he?

The scooter roared faster and faster. Now it was almost on top of Mitzi. Not slowing. Not turning.

No! I thought. Nooo!

111

A horrified scream pierced the air.

And the white, frothy waves turned bloodred as the water scooter slammed into Mitzi's body.

No! my mind screamed again. I plunged under a wave, then began swimming toward Mitzi. I had to get to her. Had to save her!

Hang on, Mitzi! I thought as I stroked through the water. I'm coming. Hang on!

My arms ached and my chest burned, but I kept fighting my way through the waves. If I can get to her in time, I can save her! I told myself. Keep going!

A strong wave swept over me, knocking me under. I surfaced quickly and glanced around. I yelled Mitzi's name over and over.

No answer.

I glanced around again. The water suddenly seemed flat. Flat and calm and empty.

And bloodred . . .

Mitzi was nowhere in sight.

I tried, Mitzi! I screamed in my mind. I just couldn't make it in time!

I tried! I screamed again.

And sat bolt upright in bed, blinking in the darkness.

Blinking away the nightmare. Another nightmare.

How many times would I have it? I wondered with a shiver of horror.

But wait.

This wasn't the same dream. Not the same at all.

A chill ran down my back as I thought about this dream.

And realized that something was very different.

This time, *someone else* ran over Mitzi.

112

It wasn't me on the water scooter. I was in the water. I was swimming to save her.

What did it mean? Why had the dream changed?

I shivered again. My clothes still felt damp and cold. Next time, don't go to sleep in a fog-drenched sweatshirt, I told myself.

I started to get up.

And froze.

A shape moved at the far end of the darkened bedroom.

The floor creaked.

The shape moved again.

Silently. Slowly.

Someone was in the room, slipping across the floor toward my bed.

"Who's there?" I cried.

Chapter 22

I jumped to the floor, my fists clenched. "Who is it?" I croaked.

The shape moved again. "It's only me," Ian's voice murmured from the shadows. "Take it easy."

"Oh, man."

I fell back across the bed and sighed. "I was ready to pound you to dust. What made you sneak in here like that anyway?"

"I wasn't exactly sneaking." Ian pulled off my windbreaker and shook it, spraying me with drops of water. "I live here too, remember?"

"Yeah." I sat up and rubbed my face.

"Anyway, it's kind of late," Ian explained. "And when I came in, I could tell by your breathing that you were asleep. So I tried to be quiet."

He made his way to the closet, flipping the light switch on the way. "Guess I wasn't quiet enough. Sorry to wake you, Adam."

"You didn't." I rubbed my face again, groaning a little. "I was already awake."

"What's wrong?" he asked as he hung the jacket up. "You okay?"

"I had another nightmare," I told him. "About Mitzi and the water scooter."

"Oh, man. Just what you need." He shook his head. "I guess what happened on the beach this afternoon brought it all back, huh?"

"I guess." I sighed. "But it was weird, Ian. The nightmare was different this time."

He narrowed his eyes at me. His expression turned to concern. "What do you mean?"

I frowned, trying to remember. I could hear the sound of the water scooter. See the flash of blue. Feel myself struggling in the choppy waves. Feel my heart pounding with fear as the scooter roared closer and closer to Mitzi.

But I couldn't hold on to the rest of the dream. The pieces kept slipping away.

"What do you mean?" Ian repeated.

"I don't know," I replied. "Something was different about it, but I can't remember now. It's gone."

"Well, at least it's over." Ian snapped off the light and dropped onto his bed. "Did you call Dr. Thall today?"

"Tomorrow," I muttered, still thinking hard about the nightmare.

"You should definitely talk to him," Ian said, yawning. "Think you can get back to sleep?"

"Maybe," I replied.

Ian was out in about thirty seconds.

I stayed sitting on my bed, staring into the shadowy room. The dream had almost faded completely now. Only the feeling stayed with me.

Something had been different about it.

But what?

Ian rolled over in his bed and began snoring softly. I heard the waves outside, and the patter of raindrops against the window.

With a sigh, I stood up and went to the dresser to find something dry to sleep in.

What difference did it make about the dream anyway? I asked myself.

So it was different. Big deal. Dreams are always weird. Always changing.

Besides, the nightmare is over, I reminded myself. For now anyway.

But when will it be over for good? I wondered, yanking off my damp sweatshirt.

When will I ever have another peaceful night?

Pounding rain woke me the next morning. Large raindrops hit the window like bullets and drowned out the sound of the ocean surf.

I sat up groggily, then squinted at the clock-radio. Ten-thirty. With a yawn, I turned the radio on.

"No chance for fun in the sun today, beach lovers!" the announcer declared cheerily. "The forecast calls for driving rain and gusty winds well into the evening. Beaches are closed to swimming, water-skiing, and all water craft. Unless you're a fish, you might as well plan to stay inside today."

116

I snapped the radio off and stretched. No work today, I thought. Good. I could use a day off.

Yawning again, I gazed around the room. Ian's bed was rumpled and empty. Already at work, I thought. The boat-rental place never closes unless there's a hurricane.

Still groggy from my troubled sleep, I stumbled into the shower. As I stood under the hot spray, bits and pieces of last night's dream flashed into my mind.

The water scooter rocking across the waves.

Mitzi falling off.

The scooter spinning around, cutting toward her through the water.

The blood.

Then what? Something different, but what?

Forget it, I told myself. Don't try so hard. Maybe it will come back to me if I just put it out of my mind.

As I shook the dream away, another image flew into my head.

Joy.

Floundering in the waves. Screaming desperately for me not to leave her alone.

Not to let her drown.

Another nightmare.

I shivered in spite of the hot, steamy shower. Could I ever put that nightmare out of my mind?

I shut the water off. Then I got dressed and hurried into the living room. My stomach had been growling since I woke up. Might as well feed it, I thought. It couldn't care less about your nightmares.

The cereal bowl still sat on the coffee table in a

puddle of milk. I cleaned it up, then opened the refrigerator.

Three cans of soda. An almost-empty carton of milk. One apple, half a chocolate bar, a piece of cheese with blue-green fuzz growing on it.

My stomach grumbled again.

You've got a choice, I thought. Stay here and starve. Or slosh through the rainstorm to the grocery store and stock up on supplies.

Definitely the store, I decided. It's better not to sit around anyway. If I sit around, I'll just think. Better to keep moving, even if I do get soaked.

Ian had borrowed my new windbreaker again. As I searched through the closet for my old one, I suddenly thought of Leslie.

She worked the morning shift at the coffee shop next to the grocery. She'd be there now.

Go see her first, I told myself. She was furious the other night, but she didn't mean what she said. Besides, I missed her. I should try to make up with her.

Do it now, I ordered myself.

Shrugging into the old jacket, I jammed a baseball cap on my head and hurried to the door.

As I reached for the knob, the phone rang. I went back to the kitchen and picked it up. "Hello?"

"Be careful," the hoarse voice whispered.

"Who is this?" I demanded. "What do you want?"

"You'll find out," the caller whispered. "Soon."

The dial tone hummed in my ear. The caller had hung up again.

Somebody's after me, I thought with a shiver. But who? Sean? Leslie? Was Leslie angrier than I thought?

At least I'm not imagining this, I told myself as I stared at the receiver. I can still hear the dial tone. I heard the voice and the words. The threat is real.

With another shiver, I hung up the phone, then left the apartment.

Outside, the wind slammed against me, almost knocking me sideways. Raindrops pelted my face and dripped down the back of my neck.

As I hurried down the path and into town, I kept glancing over my shoulder. But no one followed me.

By the time I reached the coffee shop, the rain had started to soak through my jacket. The little bell over the door jangled as I hurried inside. I slammed the door against a gust of wind, then stood there, dripping and glancing around.

Not much business this morning. Only a couple of men sat at the counter, eating eggs and chatting with the waitress.

Leslie sat in a back booth, sipping coffee and gazing out the window at the lashing rain.

She must be on a break, I thought. Perfect timing.

As I walked toward the booth, my sneakers squished loudly.

Leslie turned away from the window, and her gray eyes narrowed when she saw me.

Still angry.

Angry enough to threaten me?

I didn't know.

I stopped in front of the booth and took a deep breath. "Hi."

"Hi." She gazed at me for a couple of seconds, then

drank some coffee. "You're dripping on the table, Adam."

"Sorry." I ripped off my hat and jacket and tossed them onto the seat. Then I slid in after them and faced Leslie across the table. "Leslie, listen," I started. "About the other night—"

"Forget it," she interrupted. She tucked her dark hair behind her ears and stared out the window again.

"I don't want to forget it," I told her. "I want to talk about it. Clear the air, you know?"

"The air's already clear," she declared coldly. "You lied to me. You told me you were feeling bad, and then you went out with somebody else."

"I know," I admitted. "It was a lousy thing to do."

"No kidding."

"But I went out with her only that one time," I insisted. "I know I made a mistake. I don't even want to see her again. It wasn't that big a deal."

"Obviously not," she snapped. "Since you went out with *two* girls the very next night."

I frowned. "But Raina and Joy—"

Leslie held up her hand. "I know, I know. Old friends from high school, right?"

"Right," I agreed.

"Maybe so, but it doesn't matter." She leaned toward me across the table. "Adam, I *cared* about you. I worried about you. About your nightmares. Your hallucinations . . ."

She sighed. "I thought you were getting worse or something. And then I find you out dancing and having a great time! How do you think that made me feel?"

"Rotten," I replied.

"Good guess." She picked up her cup, then slammed it back down on the table. "Rotten and furious!"

"Okay, okay." I sighed. "I guess coming here wasn't such a great idea."

Leslie didn't speak.

I started to slide out, but then I stopped. "You know, I thought you'd be more sympathetic after what happened yesterday afternoon," I blurted out.

"Huh?" Leslie looked confused. "What happened?"

"Don't you listen to the radio or read the newspaper?" I asked. "A girl drowned in the ocean yesterday. A girl I couldn't save!"

She gasped. "Huh? Are you serious?"

"No, it's just a big joke," I said sarcastically. "Of course I'm serious. I was there! I tried to save her, but I couldn't. I was too late."

I shook my head. "You ought to know I wouldn't joke about something like that."

Leslie bit her bottom lip. "I watched the news last night," she told me. "They didn't say anything about a drowning."

She reached down beside her and slapped a newspaper on the table. "And this is today's paper. Look."

Leslie flipped the paper around and showed me the main headline: TOURIST BEACH RENTALS A RECORD HIGH.

"A drowning would definitely be the biggest story, right?" she asked.

"Let me have that!" I snatched the paper and

121

scanned the rest of the front page. No story about Joy.

I suddenly felt cold all over.

I frantically riffled through the rest of the paper, reading every headline.

No news story about Joy.

Nothing at all.

Chapter 23

"**W**hat's wrong, Adam?" Leslie demanded. "What's happening?"

I stared at her. "I'm not sure," I muttered in a shaky voice.

Ian said it was real, I remembered.

Ian said it wasn't a hallucination. It really happened.

"It—it happened," I stammered. "Leslie, it really happened. Joy drowned yesterday. For some reason, the newspaper is trying to keep it secret."

"Adam, you're not making sense!" she cried. "And your face is so pale. Are you okay? Do you feel faint? Put your head down on the table or something!"

"No, I . . . I'm okay. I mean . . ." I grabbed my jacket and hat and slid out of the booth. "Listen, I've got to get out of here, Leslie. I need some air."

She started to say something, then bit her lip. "Fine," she told me with a shrug. "Don't tell me anything. Don't explain. Just go!"

I knew she was angry all over again, but I couldn't help it. What could I tell her? How could I explain anything? I didn't *know* anything!

Throwing on my jacket, I hurried outside. The rain had let up a little. But a thick, swirling fog had rolled in.

Keeping my head down, I hurried across the road, then took the path that led to the boardwalk.

No one strolled along the wooden walkway today. I had the whole place to myself. Perfect for thinking. For figuring things out.

Except I couldn't figure *any*thing out.

Why didn't the newspaper have the story about Joy? A drowning at Logan Beach during tourist season had to be a major story.

The paper should have plastered it on the front page. The TV should have sent reporters and a camera crew. Everyone in town should be talking about it.

Why weren't they?

Ian knew about it. He said the police were there. He said the head lifeguard brought me home.

He felt so bad for me. He knew how a *second* ocean tragedy would mess me up.

Mess me up . . . mess me up . . .

My head spun. So much to think about. So much to figure out.

What about last night? I wondered. I saw Joy on the beach. Heard her speak. Found her footprints.

Except it couldn't have been Joy.

Joy is dead.

Drowned. Because of me.

I should call Dr. Thall the second I get home, I told myself.

Confused and scared, I walked on through the thick fog to the end of the boardwalk. As I started down the wooden steps, a voice called to me.

"Adam? Why, Adam?"

I spun around.

A girl stood a few feet down the boardwalk, staring at me. I couldn't see her face.

"Why, Adam?" she repeated in a sad, lost voice. *"Why did you let me drown?"*

I shook my head, blinked hard.

"Are you real?" I asked her. "Joy—is it you? Are you alive?"

She didn't answer.

The thick fog swirled around her. She faded into it, as if part of the fog.

As if made only of mist.

"I—I can't see your face," I stammered. "Joy—is it you? Please tell me. Is it you?"

"Adam . . ." She called my name again in that soft, faraway voice. *"Adam . . ."*

"Joy, I tried to save you!" I cried. "You've got to believe me!"

I held out my hand. "I tried to save you. You know I wouldn't just leave you out there. I came for you, Joy—but I was too late!"

The wind shifted. The fog swirled.

As the fog drifted around her, Joy faded into it. I squinted, struggling to see her face.

Stop her! I thought. Don't let her get away.

Go after her. Grab her arm and shake it. Go find out if she's real or not!

But I couldn't move. I stood frozen as the wind gusted again. The fog rose and fell like a thick gray blanket.

When it lifted again, she had vanished.

"Joy!" I took a running step and slipped on the rain-slick boards. I fell to my knees and scrambled up, then raced down the boardwalk to where she'd been standing.

Gone. Vanished.

The cold fog closed in again. With a shiver, I hurried to the end of the boardwalk. As I leapt down the steps, I glanced back, half expecting to see Joy behind me.

But I saw only the thick gray curtain of fog.

Shivering again, I started home. But I changed my mind and walked back to the coffee shop.

I should talk to Leslie again, I decided. Tell her everything that's been going on. She said she cared about me, didn't she? So give it a try.

But when I reached the restaurant, Leslie had already left. "She took off for some reason," the other waitress told me. "Just lit out of here like a firecracker. Didn't tell anyone where she was going."

Still furious at me, I thought glumly.

Leaving the restaurant, I hurried into the small grocery store next door and stocked up on bread and milk and stuff. A few minutes later, I staggered into my apartment with a sack of groceries in each arm.

"Ian!" I called out. "You back yet?"

No answer.

I dumped the bags on the kitchen counter and wolfed down a banana as I put the food away. My clothes were soaked again, so I hurried into the bedroom to change.

The window shades were still down and the bedroom was dark and full of shadows.

Flipping on the light, I peeled off my jacket and went to the closet.

I almost tripped as my foot hit something on the floor. I glanced down, expecting to see a stray shoe or a wadded-up towel.

"Hey—how did *that* get there?" I cried out loud.

One of my sweatshirts lay near the foot of my bed. With a confused frown, I bent down and picked it up.

And gasped as a dead sea gull dropped to the floor.

A butchered sea gull. Its head chopped off. Its body ripped open. Its feathers slick with blood.

As I stared at it in shock, I spotted a piece of paper poking out from under its blood-soaked body.

My heart pounding, I nudged the bird away and peered down at the words scrawled across the blood-spattered paper: *THIS IS YOU. YOU'RE NEXT.*

Chapter 24

You're next.

The words echoed in my mind as I walked to work the next day. The storm had passed and the sun blazed in the sky. Beachgoers hurried along the boardwalk and over the dunes, carrying coolers and towels and boogie boards.

I hardly saw their faces. Barely heard their happy, excited voices.

I couldn't stop thinking about the torn, blood-soaked sea gull and the note wrapped in one of my sweatshirts.

This is you, it said. *You're next.*

No way was that a hallucination. And neither were the threatening phone calls. I'd heard the voice on the phone. I'd held the bloody note in my hands. I'd cleaned up the dead sea gull and dumped it in the trash.

All that was real, I thought. It really happened.

Someone is definitely out to get me.

Who? I wondered. Who hated me so much that they wanted to rip me to pieces?

Leslie? Sean? The misty ghost of Joy?

Head down, I shouldered my way through the crowd and onto the beach. As I started toward the lifeguard station, someone reached out and clutched my arm.

"Sean!" I spun around, ready to fight if I had to.

But it wasn't Sean.

Instead, Raina stood there, gazing at me with a relieved expression on her face. "Adam, I'm *so* glad to see you," she declared. "I've been looking all over for you. I never got a chance to thank you. For saving my life."

"Then it really *did* happen?" I gasped.

Raina frowned. "What's that supposed to mean?"

"It's just that nobody else seems to know about it," I told her. "It wasn't in the paper or anything. I can't figure it out, Raina!"

She held on to my arm. "Listen, Adam, I have to talk to you. Can we meet later?"

"Can't we talk now?" I asked eagerly. "I really need to talk about this. I need to figure out what's going on. Raina, I really need you to explain—"

Raina shook her head. "I . . . I can't explain it," she told me. "I have to show you."

"Huh? Show me? Show me what?" I demanded. "Raina, please—"

"Meet me tonight. At seven o'clock," she replied. "At the dock, okay?"

"Okay," I agreed. "But can't we talk now, Raina? I—I keep seeing Joy. I keep hearing her—"

She shook her head tensely. "I'm sorry. Not now. Just meet me, Adam. Seven o'clock." She let go of my arm. Then she turned and ran off toward town.

I watched her for a second, my heart pounding. Why couldn't she talk to me? What did she want to show me?

Why was she being so mysterious?

Why did she seem so afraid?

At least I hadn't imagined the whole tragic afternoon.

Raina thanked me for saving her life.

It happened. It all really happened.

With a shrug, I leapt down to the sand and strode along the beach to the lifeguard station. Sean slouched in his chair. He didn't even turn his head when I climbed up.

What's his problem anyway? I wondered again as I stepped over his feet and sat down. What is he so steamed about?

I took a deep breath. "Listen, we've got to talk," I told him.

No answer.

"Hey. Sean." I turned and stared hard at him. He sat like a statue, gazing out at the beach. "Did you hear me?" I asked.

"I heard you," he muttered. "Loud and clear."

"Well?"

"Well what?"

"What's been eating you?" I demanded. "Why have you been acting so weird?"

Sean glanced at me quickly, his dark eyes snapping

with anger. "I've got nothing to say to you," he declared. Then he turned back to the beach.

"Great." I sighed in frustration. "You know, you could give me a break," I told him. "It isn't asking a lot. Not with everything else that's happening in my life."

He grunted.

"You could show a little sympathy," I said. "I mean, after what happened the day before yesterday. After Joy drowned. Did you ever think about how I feel after a thing like that?"

He grunted again. "Bad, huh?"

"It's been so rough," I admitted. "Sometimes I feel as if I'm totally falling apart."

I sensed Sean's eyes on me. I kept watching the beach.

Was I getting to him? Was he finally going to open up and tell me what was on his mind?

"And then last night," I told him, "I came home and found a bloody sea gull in my bedroom. Somebody ripped it to pieces and wrapped it in one of my sweatshirts."

I glanced quickly at Sean.

He gazed back at me, a look of total surprise on his face. "In your sweatshirt?" he asked.

I nodded. "A nice gruesome present for me. Scary, huh?"

He snapped his head back toward the ocean. "Yeah. Real scary," he agreed. Then he glanced at his watch. "It's my break time," he muttered. "Be back in twenty minutes."

I sighed again as Sean climbed down the ladder and hurried off. Had he been faking that surprise when I told him about the sea gull?

I couldn't tell.

Oh, well, I thought unhappily. I *tried* to get through to Sean. I *tried* to make things up with him.

I don't know what more I can do.

I sat back in the chair and scanned the beach and the water. Everything seemed calm. Nobody was in trouble.

The sun grew hotter, making me thirsty. As I reached into my duffel bag for some water, a shrill scream suddenly pierced the air.

I dropped the bottle and leapt to my feet, my heart pounding.

More screams echoed across the beach.

Trouble, I thought. But where?

I gripped the railing and scanned the ocean.

There! People floundering around in the water, shouting and screaming and . . . laughing.

Laughing because the wind had turned their Sunfish over and sent them sprawling into the water. Laughing as they struggled to flip the little boat right side up again.

Nobody's hurt, I told myself. Nobody's going to drown.

They're just having fun.

I let go of the railing and sank into my chair. My hand shook as I picked up the bottle of water.

Fun, I thought.

I don't even remember what that is.

I trudged up the lane to my apartment at six-thirty that evening, feeling tired and hot.

And really steamed at Sean.

After treating me like the Invisible Man all afternoon, he split early. Again.

At least nothing went wrong, I told myself. The only time I had to blow my whistle was when two kids got in an argument and started swinging their boogie boards at each other.

But something could have gone wrong, I thought. And I would have been on my own. Again.

Sean used to be a good lifeguard. But lately he was pretty irresponsible.

Shaking my head, I let myself into the apartment. I dumped my bag on the couch and headed straight to the refrigerator for some ice water.

As I reached for the handle, I heard a noise.

A soft creak.

I tensed up, but then I relaxed as I heard another creak.

It's just the squeaky floorboards in the bedroom, I thought. Ian must be home. Good. I can tell him not to borrow my car tonight, just in case he was thinking about it. After the day I'd had, I felt like driving around by myself until it was time to meet Raina.

"Ian?" Forgetting the water, I hurried across the living room. "Hey, buddy."

I stopped in the bedroom doorway—and froze.

A hulking figure stood in the room, his back to the door, one hand raised high over my bed.

What was that glinting in his upraised hand?

A butcher knife?

Chapter 25

I drew in a deep breath. "What are you *doing?*" I shouted angrily. "What's going on?"

His back still to me, the figure leapt away from the bed and stumbled into the closet door.

Furious, I charged into the room.

And stopped, stunned and terrified.

My bed had been slashed to bits. Gouged over and over and over, down into the mattress.

Pillow feathers floated in the air and drifted down onto the shredded quilt. Deep, savage slashes ripped through the sheet and into the mattress. Mattress stuffing littered the bed in thick, wadded clumps.

My sweatshirt lay on top of the sheet. Slashed to pieces.

It could have been me, I thought.

It was *supposed* to be me!

The intruder turned. Raced toward the open window.

Sunlight slanted across his face.

Sean's face!

With a cry I vaulted across the ripped-up bed, sprang through the air, and tackled him around the knees.

Sean bellowed in anger and struggled to keep his balance.

But fury made me stronger for once.

With another cry I grabbed him by the back of the neck and slammed him onto the floor.

The knife flew through the air and skittered out of reach under the bed.

"What are you *doing?*" I screamed.

Planting a knee on his back, I twisted one of his arms behind him and yanked up hard. "What do you think you're doing?"

"Adam?"

Gasping, Sean twisted and squirmed under my weight. "Let me go. Let me go. You don't—"

I yanked his arm higher. He gasped in pain again. But I didn't care.

He's the one, I thought. Threatening me with those phone calls. That torn-up bird.

Sean is the one who's been driving me nuts. Trying to terrify me!

"Why have you been doing this to me?" I demanded. "Tell me, Sean! Why are you torturing me?"

"You?" Sean's face twisted in surprise. He lifted his head from the floor and tried to look at me. "What does it have to do with *you?*"

"Don't pretend you don't know!" I shouted, pressing down harder with my knee. "I just caught you sneaking around my bedroom with a knife."

"But . . ."

"And what about those phone calls?" I reminded him. *"You're going to pay for what you did to me. Don't tell me you didn't make them!"*

"Okay, okay, I did," Sean admitted. "Let go of me. Let me up. I—I—"

"You what? You got the wrong number?" I asked sarcastically.

"No! I thought . . . I was trying to . . ."

"You were trying to torture me," I cried. "You called and threatened me. You left a bloody sea gull in the room, wrapped in my sweatshirt. And now you've slashed my bed to pieces!"

"Your bed?"

"Yes!"

Sean let his breath out in whoosh. I felt his arm go limp as he stropped struggling.

"Oh, man!" he groaned. "Adam, listen—I thought *Ian* answered the phone that night. It *sounded* like Ian! I didn't know it was you."

"Huh?" I gasped.

"That's right," Sean continued. "And that sweatshirt I wrapped the bird in? I saw Ian wearing that sweatshirt the other day, so I thought it was his. Just like I thought it was *Ian's* bed when I saw the sweatshirt lying there!"

"Ian?" I frowned, confused. "What are you talking about? What does Ian have to do with anything?"

Sean turned his head again, rolling his eyes as he tried to look at me. "I can explain, okay?" he gasped. "Just stop trying to break my arm, and I'll tell you!"

I paused. Then I shook my head. "Why should I

trust you? You broke in here with a knife," I reminded him. "Tell me why first. Then maybe I'll let you up."

"Okay." Sean sighed and lay quietly for a few seconds. "As I said, I didn't know it was you on the phone. Really. I thought it was Ian. I've been trying to warn that roommate of yours that I'm coming after him. That I'm going to pay him back!"

"Why?"

Sean tensed up again. "Because of my girlfriend!" he shouted angrily. "Ian has been sneaking out with Alyce!"

Chapter 26

"Ian is going out with Alyce?" I asked, totally surprised. "Are you sure?"

"You think I made it up?" Sean muttered. "Sure I'm sure. She met him for a movie just the other night. And last night he took her up the ocean coast to this hot new club. I followed them."

Ian and Alyce? Whoa.

Ian hadn't said a word to me about her. Sure, he told me he was seeing someone. He just didn't bother to say who.

If he had, I would have told him to forget it. Sneaking around with Alyce was playing with fire.

Letting go of Sean's arm, I removed my knee from his back and stood up.

He quickly rolled over and rose to his feet. "I guess you believe me now, right?" he asked, rubbing his arm. "About the call and the sea gull and everything. I didn't know it was you, Adam. I really thought I was doing it to Ian."

"Yeah," I told him reluctantly. "I believe you. But I don't get something—if you're so steamed at Ian, how come you've been acting as if I'm the one you hate?"

"Because he's your roommate," Sean snapped.

"So?"

He shook his head impatiently. "I figured you already knew what he was up to. That's why I've been too angry to talk to you. He's your roommate. Your friend—and I *thought* he was my friend! But I saw him with Alyce and—"

Sean broke off, gritting his teeth and clenching his fists. His eyes flashed angrily around the room.

He's looking for the knife, I thought. If he finds it and Ian walks in now, there will be major trouble.

"Sean!" I grabbed his shoulders and squeezed. "Cool it! Calm down!"

"Yeah, sure." He bared his teeth in an angry grin. "Great advice, Adam. Some guy sneaks out with my girl and you tell me to be calm?"

"Yes!" I cried. "You have to get control of yourself. Remember that story you told me about the guy in your high school?"

He nodded.

"You freaked out and beat him to a pulp, remember? You said you've been afraid of your anger ever since. Well, don't mess up again, Sean."

"You're right, I know it," he muttered, his breath coming in gasps. "But whenever I think of Ian, I feel as if I'm going to explode."

"Yeah, well, control yourself," I repeated. "I'll talk

to Ian later. I promise. But listen—I saw Ian at the Sea Shanty the other night. Not with Alyce—with another girl."

Sean stared at me skeptically.

"It's true," I insisted. "Ian likes girls, period. Not just Alyce. Okay, so he went out with her a few times. But I bet he won't stick with her. It's like . . . Ian borrows things, you know? Clothes and cars and stuff. And it's the same with girls."

"Alyce isn't exactly a thing," Sean muttered. "If she knew that's the way Ian thinks about her, she'd flip."

"Maybe she already does know. Why don't you talk to her?" I suggested.

He frowned. "I don't know . . ."

"Well, think about it," I told him. "But anyway, you've got to calm down, Sean—before you do something you'll really be sorry for."

Sean stared at me for a moment, still breathing hard. But finally I saw him begin to relax. "Yeah. Yeah," he muttered. "You're right, Adam. I'd be stupid to pull another stunt like the one in high school."

Some stunt, I thought. "Good," I told him. "Now, why don't you go home and try to relax?"

Sean nodded, but he didn't move. He just stood there as if he didn't know what to do now that he didn't have anyone to fight.

Get him out of here, I told myself. If Ian comes home, Sean will definitely have somebody to fight with.

"Why don't you go home and take it easy?" I urged.

I nudged him and pointed to the door. Finally he turned and began to walk.

"Listen to some music or watch TV or something,"

I continued as we left the bedroom. "I think there's a Dodger game on. You're a big Dodger fan, right?"

"Right."

"Great. Perfect." I pulled open the front door. "Don't worry about Ian. Really, I'll talk to him," I promised again as Sean stepped outside. "You just keep calm, okay? And think about talking it all over with Alyce."

Nodding again, Sean turned and hurried away.

I shut the door and leaned against it. Whoa! I thought again. Close call.

Sean could have killed me.

Or Ian, if Ian had come home first.

I took a shaky breath, then went back into the bedroom and started to clean up.

At least nobody's out to get me, I thought as I pulled off the shredded covers. I don't have to worry about any more whispered phone calls or dead birds.

As I flipped the mattress, a corner of it hit the radio and knocked it off the table. I picked it up and noticed the time. Quarter to seven.

Raina, I thought. I have to meet Raina at seven. Better go now.

But leave Ian a note. Warn him to stick around tonight.

I hurried into the kitchen and yanked open the junk drawer, looking for something to scribble a note on. As I fumbled through the take-out menus and broken pencils, the apartment door swung open.

"Greetings!" Ian called cheerfully.

"Hi. I'm just leaving. I was just going to write you a note," I told him.

"What's the rush?" he asked. "I walk in and you decide to split? Is it my breath or something?"

"I'm going to the dock," I told him. "But I have to talk to you later. So don't go anywhere, okay?"

"Okay. I don't have any plans anyway." Ian frowned. "But what's going on at the dock?"

"I don't have time to go into it now." I brushed past him through the door, then spun back around. "But I mean it, Ian," I warned. "I have to talk to you. Wait for me here. It's really important."

I left him standing in the doorway, still looking confused, and hurried out to my car.

Questions whirled through my head as I drove down the bumpy lane and turned onto the road leading to the dock.

Would Sean stay calm and wait for me to talk to Ian? Or would he go home and brood? Work himself up until he was ready to explode all over again?

Maybe I should have stayed and talked to Ian, I thought. Or at least given him a hint about what's wrong.

What if Ian doesn't stick around the apartment? What if he decides to go out, and Sean decides to go out, and they run into each other?

Major trouble.

I slowed the car for a second, then sped up again. Whatever Raina wanted to show me probably wouldn't take long. And Ian said he didn't have any plans.

Besides, I promised Raina I'd be there. I didn't want to let her down, not after everything that had happened.

The docks were at the far end of the beach, where the shoreline curved in and formed a big cove. Small sailboats and motorboats bumped against two of the wooden piers. Water scooters were parked at the third one.

I drove through the gate and pulled to a stop. As I got out, I glanced around.

The sun was starting to set. Most of the boats and scooters had returned for the day.

Except for a couple of fishermen tying up their boat, the docks appeared empty.

My shoes crunched loudly on the pebbly sand as I strode toward the third dock. The big water scooters bumped and thudded softly as the water rocked them against the moorings.

I shivered slightly, remembering last summer. Riding on the scooter with Mitzi. Mitzi falling off . . .

I shivered again, then spun around at the sound of footsteps.

Raina hurried toward me, her blond ponytail swinging back and forth. "Adam, hi. I'm *so* glad you came."

"No problem," I told her. "What's up?"

Raina smiled nervously. "Well . . . I'm not sure where to start."

I turned and sat down on the step that led up to the dock. "Try starting at the beginning," I suggested.

"It's so complicated," she said. "But I really do have to tell you. I mean, everything is just all wrong, Adam. I . . . we . . . thought . . ."

"Whoa." I held up my hands. "I'm not following this, Raina. What's all wrong?"

"What happened," she murmured softly.

I stared at her, confused. What is she talking about? I thought. What's going on? "Raina—"

"Okay," she interrupted. "Here goes."

Here goes what? I wondered.

Raina took a deep breath. "I owe you an apology, Adam," she declared. "And an explanation. Actually, we *both* do."

Before I could respond, Raina glanced toward the end of the dock and waved. "Come on out," she called.

Footsteps sounded on the wooden planks.

I stood up and turned around.

And gasped as Joy strode toward us from the end of the dock.

Chapter 27

No! I thought. No way! This isn't happening. I'm seeing things again!

Joy's shiny brown hair bounced up and down as she came closer. She wore white shorts and a yellow halter top.

She *looked* real.

As Joy locked her eyes on me, I shut my eyes. Shook my head.

Don't believe it, I told myself. Just stay calm and wait for it to be over.

"Adam, it's okay," Raina murmured. She gripped my hand and squeezed.

I opened my eyes.

Joy hadn't disappeared. She stepped across the boardwalk toward us.

Joy is here. And Raina is here, I told myself.

145

This isn't a hallucination.

I stood frozen, stunned, as Joy stepped up to me. She threw her arms around my neck and hugged me.

I felt the soft warmth of her arms. Felt her hair against my face and her breath on my cheek. Heard her voice.

"Adam!" she cried. "I'm so sorry!"

She *is* here, I thought in amazement. She is alive.

I pulled her arms away and stared at her. "I can't believe this," I declared in a shaky voice. "It's unreal. No—it's real! But I just can't believe it! How did you get out of the ocean? Why didn't anybody tell me?"

Joy stepped back and exchanged a glance with Raina. "We didn't tell you because—" Joy paused, blushing.

"Because we weren't supposed to," Raina finished the sentence for her.

"Huh?"

I glanced back and forth between them. "What's that supposed to mean?"

"Adam, Joy and I did something we really regret. The whole drowning scene was an act," Raina confessed. "I still can't believe we went along with it."

Joy nodded. "We feel really rotten for putting you through it, Adam."

I couldn't speak for a second. I felt totally shocked. And breathless, as if somebody had punched me in the stomach and knocked the wind out of me.

No wonder it wasn't in the newspapers. Or on the TV news.

It never happened.

"How . . . ?" I choked out. I paused and took a shaky breath. "How could you do something like that?" I demanded. "And why? Don't you know how guilty I've been feeling? Don't you know what a nightmare the last few days have been?"

"Yes!" Joy cried. "That's why we decided to tell you. It wasn't our idea to trick you, Adam."

She sighed. "That's a rotten excuse, I guess, but we never would have done something like that on our own. You've got to believe that."

"Joy is right," Raina agreed. "It was Dr. Thall's idea. He asked us to do it. He asked Ian to help, too."

"Excuse me?" I cried. "Slow down—please! You're going way too fast for me!"

I rubbed my throbbing head. "What on earth does Dr. Thall have to do with this?" I demanded.

They hesitated. Finally Joy spoke up. "We shouldn't be telling you any of this, Adam."

"But we decided we had to," Raina added. "We couldn't go on with such a terrible plan. Even if it did come from your doctor."

"What plan?" I demanded impatiently. "What does Dr. Thall think?"

"He thinks you buried the memory of what happened last summer way down deep in your mind," Joy explained. "And he wanted to try something really radical to get you to bring the memory up."

"Yeah. He decided to stage another tragedy in the ocean," Raina said. "He figured the shock of what happened with Joy and me would shake you up— shock you into remembering."

She stared hard at me. "But it didn't work, did it?" she asked sadly.

"No," I replied in a whisper, too shocked to speak. "No, it didn't work."

"Adam, we're so sorry!" Joy cried. "Really. We feel terrible. We were only trying to help. But the whole thing went too far. We knew how upset you must be. So . . . so we just had to tell you!"

Raina took my hand. "Go ahead and hate us. We deserve it."

But I didn't feel angry.

I didn't know *what* I felt. I was numb. Totally numb.

"Please, Adam, talk to us," Joy begged. "Tell us you forgive us. Talk to us about . . . everything. Maybe if the three of us sit down together, we can . . . you know . . ."

That's the one thing I *don't* feel, I thought. I don't feel like talking.

My head pounded as I tried to unscramble all the thoughts racing through it.

Get away, I told myself. I can't even think straight. I have to get away and clear my head.

Pulling away from the girls, I leapt onto the dock and began trotting out over the water.

"Adam, where are you going?" Joy cried after me. "What are you going to do?"

I didn't turn back. I kept going until I stood at the end of the dock.

"Adam, please!" Raina called. "Come back and talk to us!"

I heard them chasing down the dock after me.

No, I thought. Let me get away. Let me be myself so I can think!

Joy and Raina drew closer, shouting my name.

A wave rolled up against the pilings, spraying me with water. High tide, I thought. On my right, a yellow water scooter bumped against the swaying dock.

That's it, I decided. I'll take a ride. At least I can be by myself out on the ocean.

Fumbling with the rope, I untied the scooter and leapt onto it. As Joy and Raina ran up, I gunned the engine and roared out of the cove.

As I rode farther and farther out, my head stopped pounding and the dizziness left me. I concentrated on driving the scooter for a while, bouncing over the rolling waves and feeling the wind in my face.

But soon all the questions and thoughts crept back into my head.

Dr. Thall had set the whole thing up. I still couldn't believe it.

He told me he had some radical new treatments, but I never thought he meant something like this. Something so cruel.

But I told him I'd try anything, I reminded myself. So how could I be angry?

I shook my head, squinting against the glare of the setting sun. I wasn't angry at Dr. Thall or Joy or Raina, I realized. All they wanted to do was help.

Maybe I felt angry and upset because the fake drowning didn't work. It didn't bring back any hidden memories.

Gritting my teeth, I drove the water scooter in a wide turn, skipping and rocking over the waves.

Would I be stuck for the rest of my life like this?

Having nightmares? Seeing things? Trying to remember?

Gunning the motor again, I leapt over a high wave. The scooter slapped down hard, pitching and tossing in the water. My head snapped back.

And in the distance I saw another water scooter.

A bright metallic blue scooter, slapping and bouncing across the waves.

Roaring toward me.

The rays of the setting sun glinted off the scooter as it came closer and closer.

I squinted again, trying to see who was on it.

The wind gusted. The driver's hair blew back.

Long blond hair.

Mitzi!

But Mitzi never drove a water scooter. Not even in one of my dreams.

I shook my head, staring hard.

The water scooter drew closer, filling the air with a roar. The driver's face came into view.

Ian's face.

I started to relax, then tensed up again as I spotted Mitzi's hair whipping in the wind.

Who *is* it? I wanted to shout. Ian? Mitzi?

The blue scooter bounced over another wave, roaring closer . . . closer.

Mitzi laughed and wrapped her arms tightly around Ian.

Ian *and* Mitzi?

Ian and Mitzi?

Yes!

"Yes!" I screamed out loud. "Yes! Yes! Yes!"

That's it! That's what I've been trying to remember all this time.

I saw it! I finally pictured it!

The memory just flashed back to me. The memory just sprang up from its hiding place deep inside my mind.

Ian and Mitzi—together on the water scooter.

Chapter 28

_____

I had slowed my scooter nearly to a stop. The waves tossed me from side to side.

I was thinking so hard, I hardly noticed.

I raised my eyes, expecting the other water scooter to be gone.

Just memory. The other scooter was a bit of memory floating back to me, I thought.

But I gasped in shock when I saw it roaring toward me. Still there. Still rocking over the waves.

With only one rider.

Ian.

Ian riding toward me. Not a memory. Not a crazy picture from my mind.

Ian.

And as I watched him approach, a hot rage boiled up inside me. I gunned the engine and my scooter shot forward, pounding across the water toward Ian.

Ian, my so-called friend.

"It was you!" I screamed over the roar of the two water scooters. "It was *you!*"

Ian swerved to the side, then circled around to face me again. His face seemed tense under his tan and his eyes were filled with fear.

"You *do* remember!" he shouted. "You remember now—don't you?"

"Yes!" I screamed in fury. "After a whole year of lies, I remember *everything!*"

"I knew it! That's what I was afraid of. That's why I came after you," he yelled. "Now I have no choice!"

Ian kept shouting at me, but the roar of the two engines drowned out his voice.

I wasn't listening anyway. The memory of last summer flooded my mind, rocking my brain like the waves that rocked my water scooter.

Good old Ian, I thought bitterly. Always borrowing things. My clothes, my CDs, my car . . .

And my water scooter.

That's what he did last summer. He borrowed my water scooter.

And he borrowed my girlfriend.

He borrowed them both.

And Mitzi never came back.

"You did it!" I screamed, feeling the hot rage boil up again.

Gripping the handlebars, I spun the yellow scooter around in a tight circle until Ian and I were side by side. "You did it! You! You! Ian—you did it!"

"It was an accident!" Ian screamed hoarsely. "We

FEAR STREET SUPER CHILLER

went for a ride. Mitzi fell off. I spun around to save her and the scooter—" He broke off.

I whipped my scooter around, then raced up to his side again. "The scooter did what?" I demanded. "Tell me, Ian! I want to hear it. I *have* to hear it!"

"It ripped open her head," he shrieked. "So much blood . . . I was so scared! The water turned red and I couldn't even look anymore! I just took off and raced back to the dock."

"And I was there, wasn't I?" I demanded. "Wondering where my scooter was. Where Mitzi was!"

"Yes!" he shouted. "The minute I rode up, you knew something bad had happened. I was so freaked out, I could hardly talk. But you made me tell you. And when I did, you went into shock. You grabbed the water scooter. I tried to stop you, but you fought me off."

Yes, I thought. I remember so clearly now.

I had to find Mitzi. I had to save her, even though Ian told me she was dead.

"You threw me onto the dock. Then you jumped onto the water scooter and took off," Ian continued. "You took it way out, where Mitzi and I had been. You rode in circles. Circle after circle!"

I groaned, remembering that frantic ride. I tried to find Mitzi. I had to find her and save her.

But I was too late.

"All I could do was watch you from the dock," Ian told me. "Riding around and around and around. And then, when you came back, I couldn't believe it—you were hysterical, and you said the whole thing was *your* fault!"

Yeah, I thought. I took the blame.

"It was *your* water scooter. *Your* girl!" Ian shouted.

154

"Your mind made some kind of leap while you were circling around out there. You went crazy. You—you suddenly thought *you* had done it!"

"And you let me think it!" I screamed at him. "Didn't you? *Didn't* you?"

"Yes!" Ian admitted. "I was so scared. So terrified. I—I let you believe it!"

A whole year! I thought miserably. Ian kept his secret. He let me believe that I had killed Mitzi. He let me feel guilty for a whole year—for something I didn't do.

"You were supposed to be my friend!" I shouted furiously. "How could you do that to me? How could you let me believe I killed my own girlfriend?"

"I told you—I was scared!" he cried. The water scooter rocked beneath him. "Besides, you were so crazy with guilt, you wouldn't have believed the truth."

"How do you know?" I shouted.

We bobbed side by side. So close I could have reached out and hit him.

I wanted to. I wanted to punch him off the scooter. Watch him flounder in the water.

The way Mitzi had . . .

"You never even tried to tell me what really happened!" I cried. "You just let me keep believing that sick lie! And you got away with it. That must have felt great, huh, Ian?"

Ian shook his head. "It felt horrible. I was scared all the time, wondering . . . wondering when you'd remember. Because I knew someday you would."

Then, to my surprise, Ian gunned his water scooter engine and drove away.

At first I thought he'd left for good.

I idled along, bobbing on the waves, and watched him as he slapped across the water.

But then he turned back. And raced toward me.

As he drew closer, I heard him shouting. Screaming words I couldn't understand.

Then, over the roar of his water scooter, he came close enough for me to hear what he was saying.

"I knew you'd remember!" he screamed. "I knew it, I knew it! And now I have no choice! I can't let you go back and tell everyone!"

He's coming after me, I realized in horror.

He wants to kill me!

With a final, animal bellow, Ian slammed his water scooter straight into mine.

The impact snapped my head back.

My hands flew from the handlebars. I made a desperate grab for them—but all I caught was air.

Flying from my water scooter as if I'd been shot from a cannon, I spun through the air.

And plunged headfirst into the tossing, rocking ocean.

Chapter 29

Stunned and dizzy, I dropped deeper and deeper into the water. I had hit with such a shock, I hadn't had time to suck in air. Now my lungs screamed for air.

I opened my eyes and saw only darkness. Kicking my legs, I rolled myself over. Squinting, I could see where the water grew lighter near the surface.

Frantic for air, I swam up, rising through the water as fast as I could.

I broke the surface with a gasp, then began to tread water, sucking in big breaths of air.

The sun sat on the horizon now. Its slanting rays shimmered across the waves, almost blinding me. Squinting against the glare, I spotted my yellow water scooter.

It lay on its side, its nose almost completely submerged in the water.

Get to it before it sinks, I thought. Maybe it still has enough life to get me back to the dock.

I took one stroke. Then I pulled up short, my heart suddenly pounding in fear as I heard a buzzing sound from behind me.

The buzzing grew louder.

Rose into a roar.

I spun around, narrowing my eyes against the sun.

And saw Ian, his hair flying behind him, eyes set, expression hard. Ian, speeding across the water on the blue water scooter.

Charging straight at me.

He's not going to stop! I knew. He's coming to kill me.

He didn't mean to kill Mitzi. That was an accident. But this time . . .

The roar of the engine grew louder as Ian's scooter raced closer. I could see Ian's face clearly now, twisted with fear and anger.

I filled my lungs and dived under the water, pulling myself deeper and deeper to escape the charging machine.

Above me I heard the muffled roar of the scooter. Then the water suddenly surged, and I fought to keep it from lifting me up.

I stroked wildly, diving farther below the surface.

The noise of the scooter grew louder, then began to fade.

He had passed right over my head.

Close . . . so close . . .

But he had missed.

Go up now, I told myself. I couldn't stay down here anyway. I had to surface and make a try for the yellow scooter.

Twisting around, I began swimming up toward the surface. I couldn't hear the water scooter at all now.

Had Ian given up? Did he think he'd hit me? Did he think that I'd drowned?

I broke through the water and gulped some air. And gasped as the roar of the scooter filled my ears.

Spinning around, I saw the blue scooter slapping across the waves, racing straight toward me again.

I started to dive, then stopped myself. How many times could I dive down? Five times? Ten?

It didn't matter. Ian would always be waiting for me.

He'd play this deadly cat-and-mouse game until I didn't have any strength left.

And then he'd kill me.

He's almost on top of me! I thought. Do something. Now!

As Ian sped closer and closer, I took a deep breath and ducked under the surface. Then, kicking as hard as I could, I shot out of the water, clamped my hands around Ian's leg, and yanked him off the water scooter.

The scooter roared by, but Ian flew through the air, his mouth open in surprise as he pitched into the water beside me.

He came up quickly, choking and coughing.

I kicked and began to swim, but he came after me, shouting in fury.

Grabbing hold of my ankle, he tried to pull me back. I kicked out, but his fingers squeezed tighter.

Still shouting furiously, he got both hands around my leg. Pulling, clawing, trying to drag me under.

As I desperately tried to kick free, a strong wave suddenly lifted us up.

Ian's hands lost their grip. I heard him shout, but I couldn't see him now.

The wave dropped, slapped me back down, and tumbled over me like a waterfall.

When I rose to the surface, choking on seawater, I saw Ian about twenty feet away from me.

And I saw his water scooter.

Saw it spin around. Saw it roar toward Ian.

"Nooooo!"

Ian let out a cry and began thrashing through the water, desperate to get out of its way.

But the scooter was moving too fast.

As I watched in horror, it roared across his frantically kicking legs. Even over the roar of the water scooter, I heard Ian's shrill shriek of pain.

As he sank below the surface, the water foamed red with blood.

I struck off in his direction, swimming as fast as I could. Glancing back once, I saw the blue water scooter racing away, tossed over the waves, getting smaller and smaller, until it disappeared from sight.

"Ohhhhhhh!" Ian bobbed up again, screaming, flailing at the bloody water with both hands. "Adam—please! Help me! Help me!"

Stroking hard, spitting out water, I swam up to him. I reached out and caught one of his arms.

"Adam!" he cried. "My leg! It broke my leg!"

I glanced down at Ian's leg. It was bent at an unnatural angle. I could see white bone sticking through the skin.

"Adam, I can't swim now. I'll drown!"

I took a deep breath. "No, you won't," I told him. "I won't let you."

Taking another deep breath, I slipped one arm

around his neck. With the other arm I began pulling us both through the water, back toward the shore.

As the ambulance pulled away from the dock, Joy took my hand and held it tightly. "Are you sure you're all right, Adam?"

I nodded, still stunned and exhausted.

"Ian is probably going to be okay," Raina assured me. "I heard a couple of the paramedics talking. His leg is in bad shape, and he lost a lot of blood. But you saved him, Adam. You saved him."

Yeah, I thought. I saved the guy who let me live a lie for a year. A year of total horror. He watched me, knowing what I went through.

Knowing what really happened last summer.

But I had to save him. No matter what, I couldn't let him die out there.

"You should go home now," Joy said softly. "Get some rest. Want us to drive back with you?"

"Thanks, but I kind of want to be alone," I said. "I need to think about things."

I smiled at them both. "But listen, don't feel bad about the fake drowning anymore. It worked. Dr. Thall was right. It did help to shock my memory. It helped me figure out what really happened last summer. I'll see you tomorrow and explain it all, okay?"

Joy and Raina both gave me a hug. I watched them walk side by side away from the dock.

I trudged over the sand to my car, so tired I could hardly pick my feet up. As I stumbled along, two people stepped out from the shadows.

Sean and Alyce.

"Hey—I saw them taking Ian away," Sean said. "What a mess! You okay?"

I nodded again. I didn't want to discuss Ian with him right now.

"Well, listen, I owe you one," Sean went on. "I took your advice and talked to Alyce."

Alyce smiled. "Sean acted almost human. I guess I have you to thank for that, Adam."

"Hey—almost human? Is that supposed to be a compliment?" Sean griped.

He turned to me, and his expression changed. "You're probably right about me having to do something about my temper." He shrugged. "Who knows? Maybe I'll go see your shrink. Couldn't hurt, right?"

"Right." I had to smile. "Couldn't hurt."

When I let myself into my apartment, a deep, rumbling noise almost made me jump. But I caught myself in time.

Relax, I thought. It's only the refrigerator. Nobody's in here. Nobody is out to get me anymore.

Nobody ever *was* out to get me.

Except Ian.

I crossed the room and collapsed onto the couch. Exhausted, I closed my eyes. Ian's face immediately flashed into my mind. Ian thrashing in the ocean. Eyes wide with fear and pain. Mouth open in a scream as he pleaded with me to help him. Not to let him drown.

And I didn't, I thought. I got him out. I brought him to shore.

If only he had told me the truth, I thought.

I tried to relax. Maybe I'll stop seeing things now. Maybe the nightmares are finally over too.

And then a figure floated silently into the room.

Chapter 30

"Leslie!" I cried. "Am I imagining you?"

She laughed. "No. I let myself in."

Leslie gazed across the room at me with her serious gray eyes. She wore a short green dress and her dark hair curled around her face.

She looked great.

"I heard about Ian," she told me. "Are you okay?"

I stood up and walked over to her. "Yes. I'm okay now," I said. "But are you really here? I'm not imagining you, am I?"

Leslie didn't speak. She stepped up to meet me and kissed me softly on the lips.

"What do you think?" she asked, tilting her head. "Was that a real kiss? Or did you imagine it?"

I slipped my arms around her waist and pulled her close. "I don't really care," I said. And I kissed her again.

DEAR READERS:

I'm writing to tell you about a very special Fear Street, coming up next month. This story has so many scares and surprises, it took me TWO books to tell it all!

I hope you will come with me to FEAR HALL. That's the creepy campus dorm built many years ago by the Fear family.

Hope and her roommates live in Fear Hall. They're good students and they get along really well. They have just one little problem—they're majoring in murder!

Life at Fear Hall can be a SCREAM! I hope you will join me for both books. I had so much evil fun writing them, I scared MYSELF!

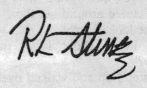

THE NIGHTMARES
NEVER END . . .
WHEN YOU VISIT

**Turn the page for a sneak peek
at the next Fear Street . . .**

FEAR HALL: THE BEGINNING

THE NIGHTMARE
NEVER END...
WHEN YOU VISIT

WELCOME TO FEAR HALL. . . .

All the books you read about Ivy State College tell you that it's a quiet, pretty school. Not a big university, but a good school, with friendly instructors and about three thousand students from all over the country.

That's what the books and pamphlets tell you.

They don't tell you about Fear Hall.

My name is Hope Mathis, and I can tell you about Fear Hall—because I live there.

Fear Hall is the biggest dormitory at Ivy State. It's a tall, brick building with ivy running down the sides and curling into some of the windows.

Fear Hall is only a block from The Triangle. That's the big, grassy area in the middle of campus.

But even though our dorm is so big, it's only half full.

Know why?

Because of its bad reputation.

As soon as I moved my stuff into room 13B, the other girls started telling me stories about Fear Hall. Frightening stories.

They told me that the dorm was named after Duncan Fear. He donated the money to have it built. He's a guy from a rich family that lives in Shadyside—a town about fifty miles from here.

The Fear family is supposed to be unlucky, or evil, or something. And I guess a lot of unlucky and weird things have happened in my dorm.

I don't mean strange sounds at night. Creaking doors. Stuff like that. I mean things like girls seeing ghosts. And creatures floating through the halls. And kids disappearing.

I'm not sure if I believe any of the stories. But the campus store sells T-shirts that say: I SURVIVED FEAR HALL.

Sure, it's a joke. But a lot of kids at Ivy State don't think it's funny. And I think that all the jokes and weird stories are the reason why the dorm is only half full.

Some floors are totally empty. But my little room on the thirteenth floor is crowded enough.

I have three roommates—Angel, Eden, and Jasmine.

We're all freshmen. We've been here only a month. But we're like a family. Because we all knew each other in high school. It's a good thing we're so close. Because the four of us are squeezed into a room that's barely big enough for one!

Should I describe my roommates?

Well, maybe I should start with me. I'm about five seven. Not too tall, not too short. I have blond hair—

long and straight, because I don't like to spend a lot of time on it.

I have light brown eyes and an okay face. I think it's a little too round. And I think my eyes are too close to my nose.

Whatever. I'm not the kind of girl who spends a lot of time gazing into mirrors. Not like Angel.

Angel is skinny and blond and very hot looking. The guys all go nuts for her. They all think she's really sexy. And she slinks around in tights and midriff tops, even though it's fall.

Eden is sort of the opposite of Angel. She's kind of plain and grungy. You know. Lots of flannel shirts from L.L. Bean. No makeup at all. She has light brown hair, very curly, that just bounces around on her head.

Unlike Angel, Eden doesn't seem interested in the boys here at Ivy State. I've never even seen her *talking* to a boy.

Eden calls Angel "Miss *Purrr*fect." I don't think Angel likes it. But she and Eden get along okay—for opposites.

Jasmine is the quiet one. I've known her for three years, but I can barely tell you a thing about her. She's very shy. It's almost impossible to get her to talk about herself.

She's very pretty. She has bright green eyes that crinkle up when she smiles. And she has wavy, straw-colored hair that falls perfectly down past her shoulders.

But Jasmine is so shy and self-conscious—I don't think she knows how pretty she is. She doesn't go out much. She's the brain in our room. Always has her face in a book.

Anyway, that's our little group. The four friends of 13B.

We're all very different. But we were really happy. Until the night the trouble started.

I'll never forget that night. Hands shook me awake—roughly.

Still half asleep, I opened my eyes. Squinted up in the darkness. My eyes stopped at my clock radio. One in the morning.

The hands shook me again. I sat up in bed.

"Darryl—what are you doing here?" I whispered. My throat was clogged from sleep.

Darryl is my boyfriend. He leaned close. His hands still gripped my shoulders. I could smell beer on his breath.

I glanced around to see if he had awakened my three roommates. No.

"Darryl—" I whispered. "Get back to your room. You know boys aren't allowed on the girls' floors after ten."

He didn't move. His hands tightened on my shoulders. Even in the dim light from the window, I could see the fear on his face.

"Hope, I'm in big trouble," he said.

I sat up and squirmed out from under his hands. I swallowed hard. "Trouble?" My mouth felt so dry.

Darryl nodded. A hoarse cry escaped his throat. "You've got to help me," he said, his voice cracking.

I raised a finger to my lips. "Shhhh. You'll wake up Angel, Eden, and Jasmine."

"I don't care who I wake up," he cried. "I mean—I'm in trouble, Hope. I—I did something terrible."

I felt a chill roll down my back. The skin on my

arms prickled. I stood up and pulled down the long, white cotton nightshirt I was wearing.

I pushed back my hair. The room was cold. But I felt drops of sweat on my forehead. "What did you do?" I demanded.

His pale blue eyes flashed, gray in the dim light.

"I followed you," he confessed. "I followed you tonight. I saw you out with that guy Brendan."

I gasped. "But that wasn't me!" I protested. "I didn't go out with Brendan. Angel did."

Darryl grabbed me. His fingers tightened around my arms. "Don't lie to me!" he shrieked. "I *saw* you!"

"Let go," I whispered. "Please, Darryl—"

He has a terrible temper. Sometimes he really scares me. One second he'll be perfectly in control. The next second he'll be in a screaming rage. A total lunatic.

He can also be very understanding. Very kind.

I met Darryl back in high school. He rescued me. From a guy named Mark. But that's a very long story.

I was so glad that Darryl decided to come to Ivy State. He and my three roommates have really helped me make the big jump from high school to life at college.

If only he wasn't so jealous. So possessive.

He never wants any other guy to even *look* at me! At first, I was flattered. But when I saw how jealous Darryl became . . . when I saw his temper rage out of control . . . I knew I'd have to be careful.

I knew that Darryl could be someone to fear.

"Darryl—let go," I pleaded. "That wasn't me you saw with Brendan. It was Angel. I swear."

He let out a sigh. "I did something terrible," he whispered.

"What?" I demanded. "What did you do?"

His pale eyes locked on mine. "I carved him, Hope," Darryl whispered. "I carved him."

About R.L. Stine

R.L. Stine is the best-selling author in America. He has written more than one hundred scary books for young people, all of them bestsellers.

His series include *Fear Street*, *Ghosts of Fear Street* and the *Fear Street Sagas*.

Bob grew up in Columbus, Ohio. Today he lives in New York City with his wife, Jane, his teenage son, Matt, and his dog, Nadine.